THE EGYPTIAN

MIRROR

THE EGYPTIAN MIRROR

Michael Bedard

pajamapress

First published in Canada and the United States in 2021

This is a first edition.

10 9 8 7 6 5 4 3 2 1

www.pajamapress.ca   info@pajamapress.ca

The publisher gratefully acknowledges the support of the Canada Council for the Arts and the Ontario Arts Council for its publishing program. We acknowledge the financial support of the Government of Canada through the Canada Book Fund (CBF) for our publishing activities.

Library and Archives Canada Cataloguing in Publication

Title: The Egyptian mirror / Michael Bedard.

Names: Bedard, Michael, 1949- author.

Identifiers: Canadiana 2019021127X | ISBN 9781772781106 (softcover)

Classification: LCC PS8553.E298 E49 2020 | DDC jC813/.54—dc23

Publisher Cataloging-in-Publication Data (U.S.)

Names: Bedard, Michael, 1949-, author.
Title: The Egyptian Mirror / by Michael Bedard.
Description: Toronto, Ontario Canada : Pajama Press, 2020. | Summary: "Thirteen-year-old Simon and his friend Abbey become embroiled in mysterious and fantastical events surrounding the ancient Egyptian mirror of Simon's elderly neighbor, Mr. Hawkins. When the old man dies, a suspicious couple claiming to be his relatives moves in. Simon, who has been plagued with a strange illness since first looking into the mirror, retrieves it from Mr. Hawkins' hiding place and seeks the help of a museum curator to unravel a dark spell tied to its original owner and to Mr. Hawkins' so-called niece" -- Provided by publisher.
Identifiers: ISBN 978-1-77278-110-6 (paperback)
Subjects: LCSH: Magic – Juvenile fiction. | Amulets, Egyptian – Juvenile fiction. | Detective and mystery fiction. | BISAC: JUVENILE FICTION / Legends, Myths, Fables / General. | JUVENILE FICTION / Paranormal, Occult & Supernatural.
Classification: LCC PZ7.B464Gir |DDC [F] – dc23

Cover design—Rebecca Bender
Text design—Lorena Gonzalez Guillen

Pajama Press Inc.

469 Richmond St. E Toronto, ON M5A 1R1

Distributed in Canada by UTP Distribution
5201 Dufferin Street Toronto, Ontario Canada, M3H 5T8

Distributed in the U.S. by Ingram Publisher Services
1 Ingram Blvd. La Vergne, TN 37086, USA

Printed in Canada

For Ann

I felt my life with both my hands
To see if it was there —
I held my spirit to the Glass,
To prove it possibler —
                                                Emily Dickinson

PART I
TAKING DINNER TO MR. HAWKINS

The ancients believed that all people were born double...

-Randall Hawkins, *Soul Catchers*

1

Not everyone is the same. People are different. Either they start out that way, or they are shaped by the things that happen to them. Not everything happens now. Some things happened long ago, and cast their shadows down through time. Others are contained within the short span of a life, cupped like sand in the palms of one's hands.

When Simon looked back on the year he turned thirteen, it was a memory shaped by the mysterious illness that struck him that year—and all the mysteries that seemed to follow from it, and somehow be part of it. So that each year now, when the turning of the seasons woke the old symptoms again like a memory in the bone, that time flooded back whole in his mind. And suddenly he was there again, on the bright summer day it all began, taking dinner to Mr. Hawkins.

The tray shook in his hands as he carried it down the walk that day. The dishes chattered, and the saucer trembled on its perch atop the cup of steaming tea. Down at the end of the street a diamond had been chalked on the road, and a baseball game was in full swing. He could hear the guys talking to one another as he stepped through the break in the hedge onto the sidewalk—deep center field.

Blinded by the glint of the sun off the tray, he felt for the edge of the sidewalk with the toe of his shoe. As he stepped off the curb he heard the crack of the bat and prayed the ball wasn't headed his way. These were big guys, and when they got into a ball, there was no telling where it might go. He'd seen them scatter like sparrows more than once that summer at the sound of breaking glass. At the beginning of June, they'd broken a second floor window at the side of the Hawkins' house.

Two weeks back, Mr. Hawkins took it into his head to mend the broken window. Simon had been home sick from school that day and saw the whole thing from his bedroom window. He watched the old man haul the long wooden ladder from behind the house on his shoulder and position it below the broken window; watched him slowly scale it as it wobbled and waved like a licorice whip. While perched high atop the rickety old thing, cutting away the caulking from around the broken window, he took a fall and crashed down into the flowerbed below.

Simon called down to Mom. She told him to keep an eye on Babs and tore across the street. She found the old man lying in a heap, his head bleeding, his leg twisted under him at an angle no leg was meant to take. She called an ambulance and stayed with him till it came.

He was in the hospital over a week. As well as breaking his leg, he'd suffered a concussion, and they wanted to keep him under observation. Mom visited him every day while he was there, for he had no family she knew of, and since his wife Eleanor had died two years ago, he was alone in the world.

Mom's ties with the Hawkins family ran deep. She'd grown up on this street. Her dad and Mr. Hawkins had been childhood friends. So when Granddad died last fall, and she and Dad decided to trade the store-top apartment where they'd been living for the small frame house she'd been brought up in, it had been like moving home.

The ball smacked down on the road right in front of Simon and skittered past him up the street. He was so startled he nearly dropped the tray.

"Hey, Simon, get that, will you?" shouted one of the guys.

"Can't," he called over his shoulder, and kept walking.

At the beginning of the summer holidays, at Mom's urging, he'd ventured down to the end of the street one day to ask if he could play. He was younger than they were, and short for his age. They looked him up and down and snickered. One of them, a kid called Joe whose mom ran a home daycare across the street, seemed to be their leader. He quieted the others with a glance, clapped his arm around Simon's shoulder, and said he could be outfielder.

His job as outfielder was to station himself down the

street and call out when cars were coming, tramp through gardens, shake bushes, and leap fences—looking for balls. A few weeks back, Joe hammered a ball that sailed high and far and came down in the lilac bushes inside the Hawkins yard. Joe stood at the plate, his cap skewed to one side, the sunlight dancing off the stud he wore in one ear. Since losing the ball that broke the Hawkins window, he'd been forced to use his prize ball, autographed by his hero, Jesse Barfield. Barfield was leading the American League in home runs, and Joe was not about to give up easily on the ball.

He gave Simon a long look and nodded his head in the direction of the Hawkins yard. Simon crossed the road on shaky legs, scooted across the old man's grass, and slipped in through the gate. As he frantically rooted around in the lilac bushes, searching for the ball, he heard a creak behind him. The back door opened, and out came Mr. Hawkins, cursing and waving his cane.

Simon thought he would die. But suddenly the old man stopped—stopped dead in his tracks and stared, as if he'd seen a ghost. And Simon tore off through the gate without the ball. Joe hadn't quite forgiven him for that.

He ran past Simon in pursuit of the rubber ball they'd been using since then. Scooping it from the curb, he tossed it toward home plate.

"Where you headed with that, Simon?" he said, eyeballing the tray.

"Taking it to Mr. Hawkins," he said, like it was something you did every day.

"Really," said Joe, falling in step with him as he crossed the road. "Say, is that blueberry pie?" He leaned over the tray and took a big sniff. "I love blueberry pie," he said, and without a word of warning he took a swipe at the pie.

Simon swung the tray away. The saucer perched on top of the teacup lifted off like an alien spacecraft. It spun in a lazy arc through the air and came crashing down on the sidewalk in front of the Hawkins house.

"Sorry," said Joe, "I was just playing with you, man." And he jogged off to rejoin the game.

Simon stared down at the broken saucer. It was from the good set in the china cupboard. Mom had taken it out especially for Mr. Hawkins. Some of the tea had slopped over the edge of the cup onto the tray. It ran in rivulets around the cup and plates. Joe had tweaked off the tip of the pie, and a bit of the filling had fallen onto the tray, turning the tea that ran by it blue.

He toed the broken saucer to the edge of the sidewalk and nudged it out of sight under the scruffy grass. He thought about turning back, then thought better of it. Taking a deep breath, he started up the walk to the Hawkins house.

The wind chime played its random music as he approached, like his baby sister Babs at her xylophone. Sunlight danced off the shards of mirror glass. The wisteria vine that snaked up the porch post and looped across the beam below the eaves was in flower, its gnarly old branches decked with purple blooms.

One of the treads wobbled under him as he started up the stairs. At the far end of the porch a wooden porch swing sat heaped with bundled newspapers. The ancient doorbell was on a twist handle set in the center of the door. There was no way he could turn it without putting down the tray. A white wicker table stood below the large front window that looked onto the porch. He set the tray down on it. The window was dark, the interior dim through a mist of sheers.

To the right of the door the mailbox dangled from one screw. A mirror was mounted on the brick above it, set in an octagonal wooden frame decorated with Chinese symbols. It was meant to ward off evil spirits, Mom said. The spirits couldn't stand to see their reflection in the mirror, so they stayed away. Some of the silvering had flaked off the mirror's back, and a bit of the brick wall behind showed through.

He gave the bell a twist. The tumblers, slack with age, made a feeble ring. But before he'd taken his hand away, the door opened, and he stood face to face with Mr. Hawkins.

They eyed one another a moment, without a word. The old man looked smaller than he had that day in the yard. His keen old eyes studied Simon over the top of the small round glasses perched on the end of his nose. The lines on his face looked chiseled in stone. He wore a satin dressing gown with a purple sash. His left leg was in a cast up over the knee. He leaned heavily on a wooden cane with a carved handle in the shape of a snake's head.

Simon prayed the old man wouldn't recognize him as the boy in the lilac bushes that day. "I'm—"

"Simon. Yes, Jenny's son."

He'd never heard anyone call his mother that before. It was 'Jennifer.' Sometimes, if Dad was feeling particularly affectionate, 'Jen.' But *never* 'Jenny.'

"I brought you some dinner," he said, and watched the old man glance down at his empty hands. "It's on the table," he said. "I put it down so I could ring—"

"Remarkable," said the old man, "Absolutely remarkable." And hitching himself around awkwardly with his cane, he motioned Simon to follow him into the house.

2

"The spitting image," Mr. Hawkins muttered as he hobbled down the hall. Waggling his cane behind him, he disappeared through a doorway on the right.

"This way, young man. This way. Mustn't let that food get cold."

Mom had warned Simon that the old man could be a little prickly. She had failed to mention crazy.

The dishes juddered on the tray as he followed after him. The scent of cut flowers and furniture polish hung in the air, overlaying the deeper, more pervasive smell of age. A worn runner ran the length of the hall, then bumped itself up the stairs and disappeared into the shadows of the second floor. A cluster of mirrors on the wall caught at his reflection as he went by. Mom had told Simon about the old man's mirror collection. She said when she was young the kids used to call him Mr. Mirror.

At the end of the hall, a vase of roses stood on a table in front of a window that looked out on the Hawkins side yard. A drift of petals lay scattered around it. A few had settled on a pair of scuffed balls nestled against the base of the vase. One was the Barfield ball. Simon swallowed hard and turned into the room where Mr. Hawkins had disappeared.

"Forgive the state of things," said the old man. "My life's all topsy-turvy since this fall." Supporting himself on his cane, he was fumbling with a large book on the bottom shelf of a bookcase on the wall opposite the door.

"Oh, blast this bloody leg," he cursed, and gave the cast a sharp smack with his cane as he abandoned the attempt. He made his way over to a padded armchair and sat heavily down.

"Don't linger there in the doorway, lad. Come set that down here." He pointed to a metal TV table by his chair.

As he put the tray down on the table Simon noticed another like it beside a neighboring armchair piled high with books. Between the spilled tea and the ravaged pie, the dinner looked a disaster. He shifted the table in front of the old man.

"It was Eleanor started us watching the evening news while we ate dinner," said Mr. Hawkins with a sidelong glance at the armchair next to his. "Disgusting habit, really. But I can't seem to give it up."

He turned his attention to the tray. "Is that blueberry pie you've got there?"

"Yeah. My mom baked it today."

"Wonderful." He didn't say a word about the state of it, or the puddle of blue tea the plate sat in. He just quietly removed the cover from the dinner plate and leaned down to smell the meal Mom had put together for him—meatloaf with mashed potatoes and spinach.

"Ah, home cooking. How I miss that. Everything I eat these days comes from a box or a tin." He took the knife and fork from the soggy napkin they were wrapped in and tucked into the meal.

"Thank you for carrying this over for me, Simon. I'm sorry for any trouble it may have caused you."

"I had a little accident on the way."

"Sometimes, crossing even the quietest street can be a dangerous thing," said the old man, with a glance his way. "Now switch that fool thing on, will you? Then I want you to fetch a book for me. I've got something to show you."

A portable TV sat on a wheeled stand by the wall. Simon went over and switched it on. The news was just coming on. The picture was poor; the newscaster looked like he was reading the news in the midst of a snowstorm.

"Give it a smack. That sometimes does the trick."

Simon smacked the set once, then a second time with feeling—to no effect.

"Don't worry about it. It's just background noise, anyway," said the old man. "Now, on that bottom shelf over there, there are some photo albums." He pointed to the bookcase he'd been standing at when Simon came into the room.

"Eleanor was a demon for photo albums. It's the third from the right. The one with the blue cover. Yes, that's it. Bring it over here and sit down there beside me. You'll have to clear those things off Eleanor's chair. She won't mind."

It was an odd thing to say, and Simon gave him a look as he lifted the stack of books off the seat of the chair and looked for a place to put them down. The room was in a state of turmoil. It looked as if things had been brought from other places in the house and dropped here. The dining room table at the far end of the room was cluttered with books and papers, pill bottles, and piles of folded clothes. A camp cot had been set up beside it. It seemed the old man was sleeping down here.

Finally, he set the books on the floor and sat down in the chair, the album on his lap. The chair was upholstered in worn red velvet. Doilies had been pinned to the arms to hide the wear. A fringed shawl was draped over the back. A pair of black brocade slippers peeked their toes out from under the skirt of the chair. It was as if Eleanor had popped out on an errand and would momentarily return.

"Switch on the light, so you can see," said Mr. Hawkins. "It's somewhere in there. You'll know it when you come to it. Two boys, sitting on the porch steps out front." He went back to his meal, one leg flung stiffly forward in its cast, his cane propped against the arm of his chair.

Simon flicked on the lamp by the chair and opened the photo album. Across the room the newscaster battled on through the blizzard.

He began flipping through the album. It was all old family photos—black and white prints held in place with gummed corner mounts. Many were studio shots, stiff and formal. There were gaps here and there where pictures had fallen out or been removed. He turned the pages as carefully as he could, but the thick old photos kept threatening to pop free.

The old man glanced over. "Further, Simon, further. I'm still too young there."

It was deadly dull, looking at page after page of dour old strangers. His attention kept drifting from the album to the room around him. The fine old furniture; the books lining the walls—more books than he'd ever seen in a house before; the mirrors that met his gaze wherever he turned, some hardly looking like mirrors at all—ancient things of metal, their surfaces shrouded with corrosion, their secrets shut away.

One in particular kept drawing his attention. It hung on the wall opposite the chair where he sat. It was a bronze mirror, about the size of the plate Mr. Hawkins' dinner was on. Round like that, though slightly flattened—the shape the sun has as it hangs on the horizon before it sets. The handle was in the form of a woman with the head of a lion, her arms raised above her head to support the disc. Unlike the other metal mirrors around it, this one shone.

The boy in the photos began to change. Now he was a gangly boy with a book, sitting cross-legged in a chair, staring up into the camera as if he'd been called from somewhere far off—the same boy, but different somehow, as though a light had been flicked on inside. The photos, too, had changed. There were suddenly more outdoor shots. Street scenes of the neighborhood a lifetime ago: the Hawkins house sitting prim and proud on its little rise of land, large old cars huddled like cattle along the curb, the fence at the end of the street just half as high as the one there now.

"There," said Mr. Hawkins, startling him as he turned the page. "Right there. The spitting image."

It was a black and white shot of two boys sitting side by side on the front porch steps of the Hawkins house, smiling at the camera. They wore T-shirts, jeans, and sneakers, and had the look of boys in on a secret. One was the boy from the other photos. But it was his companion who caught Simon's attention—a boy who looked so much like Simon that it might have been him sitting there on the porch steps. He looked up, stunned.

Mr. Hawkins let out a chuckle.

"That's your granddad and me," he said. "My mother took that photo of us with the camera I'd been given for my birthday that summer. It captures the two of us perfectly. And the two of *you* could be twins.

"We shot everything in sight that summer. When we ran out of things in the neighborhood, Davey suggested we try the museum. He'd been there with his class that year, and he had the notion of taking a photo of the mummy in its tomb. It was strictly forbidden, of course, but we were young, and we were on a mission. So off we went. I still recall the shock of delight when I looked up under the lid of the mummy's coffin and saw the wonderful things that had been painted there—as bright as the day they were done—nearly four thousand years ago.

"We shot a lot of other things there that day, as well. Ancient things unearthed from the desert sand. Among them mirrors much like these." He gave a nod in the direction of those on the wall. "Dimmed and corroded by time, but magical still. Windows onto vanished worlds. I imagined all the things they'd reflected lay somehow hidden in them still.

"That was the start of it. I devoured everything I could find on early archaeologists and the excavation of ancient civilizations. I reveled in the exploits of Caledon's own Edmund Walker—the fantastic treasures he brought back from his digs in Egypt and donated to the Caledon museum in its early days. I longed to feel that thrill of discovery. And right then and there I knew what I wanted to be. So I owe a great debt of gratitude to your granddad, Simon. He helped set me on my way."

Simon looked down at the double looking back at him.

"Take it," said Mr. Hawkins.

"I couldn't."

"Nonsense. It's not doing any good shut up in there." He leaned over, plucked it out, and handed it to him. "Now put this old thing back."

Simon returned the album to its place on the shelf. As he was walking back to his chair his eye was drawn to the mirror that had caught his attention before. He saw himself reflected in its ghostly surface, behind him the empty chair where he'd been sitting, the books stacked beside it on the floor. It was not like looking in an ordinary mirror. Everything was murky and dim, steeped in mystery.

He was about to turn away when a ripple of darkness appeared at the mirror's rim. It spread across the surface, till the whole reflection was swallowed by it. As it spread, it snuffed out all sound, and he found himself wrapped in a vast silence. It was as if he were looking down into a dark pool, and some dim shape was rising slowly to the surface. He saw a face forming, wide eyes peering up through the murk.

"Simon?" came a voice from far away.

The darkness dissolved, and the mirror went back to what it had been.

"What is it?" said Mr. Hawkins, looking at him curiously.

"Oh, nothing," said Simon, and gathered up the dishes to go.

"Tell your mother the dinner was delicious. I thank her very much."

"Thanks for the picture," said Simon.

"Not at all," said the old man. "It's been like a bit of the past come back to life. You can let yourself out. Just pull the door closed behind you."

"And one more thing," said Mr. Hawkins as Simon turned to go. "You may take those balls in the hall with you when you go. Give them back to the boys they belong to. It may help ease your crossing if you come again—as I hope you will. Next time, I'll set you to work."

3

"How did it go?" asked Mom as she dried Babs' wet hair with a towel after her bath. Babs was two and could be a bit of a handful. She didn't like having her hair dried and was putting up a fuss.

"Fine. He really liked the dinner. He said to thank you."

"See, I told you he was nice." After the incident with the ball in the bushes, Simon had been nervous about taking dinner to Mr. Hawkins when Mom asked him.

"He gave me a picture of Granddad and him when they were kids," he said, showing her the photo.

Mom leaned over and took a peek. "My, you look like him," she said.

"My wan dee picter too, Dimon," wailed Babs as she squirmed to escape.

"Okay, you can see it after you get your pajamas on," he said. "But you have to be a good girl for Mamma now."

He took the picture to his room. It was a small room, as were all the rooms in the narrow old house. The floor creaked, and the ceiling sloped. But with a big bay window overlooking the street, it was airy and bright. And it beat looking out on the rusty fire escape and the dingy laneway at the old place.

He looked over at the Hawkins house, directly opposite theirs. It was the oldest house on the street, and the grandest, sitting on a piece of property twice as large as the rest, with a wide swath of lawn and garden running down one side and wrapping around the back.

He heard Babs chattering away through the wall as Mom readied her for bed. For the first couple of months after they moved in, the bedroom beside his had been Mom and Dad's. Babs had shared it with them, her crib crammed into the corner at the foot their bed. But Babs was a restless sleeper and Dad an early riser—and with her constant stirring and waking, nights became an endless drama.

For the sake of their sanity, Mom and Dad moved down to the living room to sleep on the sofa bed. The bed frame bumped against the legs of Granddad's old upright piano, and the rocking chair spent its nights in the kitchen with the coffee table. Dad routinely stubbed his toe on them as he stumbled about, half-asleep, at the crack of dawn, getting ready for work.

The situation was less than perfect, as Mom put it. The rooms were cramped, the fuses blew, the old pipes shuddered in the walls, and the wind whistled through the leaky windows. But it was a house, and it was theirs. There were many families far worse off than them.

As he tucked the photo in the frame of his dresser mirror Simon glanced at his reflection in the glass and remembered the odd experience with the mirror at Mr. Hawkins' house. Babs came padding into the room in her pajamas, clutching her brush in her hand, her hair all spikey wet.

Mom popped her head through the doorway. "Would you mind, Simon? She *insists*. It seems you have the magic touch."

Babs dragged the desk chair over in front of the dresser and scrambled up onto it. She took a quick peek at the picture she'd wailed to see, but was instantly sidetracked by the sight of her reflection in the mirror. She tucked her chin down coyly against her shoulder and looked at herself.

"Who's that in there?" Simon said, taking the brush from her hand.

As he drew it through her hair she gazed transfixed into the glass, not even flinching as he tugged through the tangles. She knew well enough who that was in there, having *her* hair brushed, feeling the tug of the brush, the prickle of the bristles against *her* scalp. That was Babs.

She hadn't always known that. Not long ago, she hadn't a clue who the girl in the mirror was, or how she'd gotten in there. Last winter, when they first moved in, Mom would often put Babs in the playpen in the living room with some toys, while she worked in the kitchen in the next room, keeping an eye on her through the door.

A full-length mirror in a hinged wooden stand stood near the playpen. It had belonged to Granddad, one of the many things of his that shared the house with them now. In no time at all Babs made friends with the little girl who lived in the mirror. She babbled away to her and didn't seem to mind that the little girl never answered back. She offered her toys through the bars of the playpen. But the little girl couldn't seem to hang on to them, and let them all fall to the floor.

It wasn't long before Babs considered the playpen a prison, and screamed blue murder after more than a few minutes in it. Her playmate seemed unhappy too. They clearly had a lot in common.

So the first thing she did when she was set free was go to visit the little girl. But when she tried to crawl into the mirror where she lived, it tilted away. And when she searched behind it, there was no one there. After several futile attempts, she decided the little girl was being deliberately difficult—and wanted nothing more to do with her. She crawled past the mirror without so much as a glance in her direction.

This went on for some months. Then one day last spring, she was in the living room by herself, being very quiet—never a good sign. Simon went to see what she was up to. He found her sitting on the floor in front of the mirror. She touched her mouth, and watched the girl in the glass touch hers. She touched her eyes, then her nose, and watched intently as the little girl did the same.

"Who's that?" he asked, pointing to the mirror.

"Babs," she said. But there was a hint of doubt in her voice, some mystery to it she couldn't fathom.

Maybe the mystery never really went away, thought

Simon, as he drew the brush through her damp hair and watched his mirror self do the same.

"I'll take that over," he said as Mom prepared the dinner tray for Mr. Hawkins the next day.

"Are you sure?"

"Positive." And from then on it was simply understood that Simon would carry dinner across to the old man. Now that they had the balls back again, Joe and the gang grew accustomed to his daily trek to the old man's house, and let him be.

Since his accident, Mr. Hawkins had all but abandoned going upstairs. The cumbersome cast made the task too much for him.

"Takes me half the day to get up there, and the other half to get back down," he complained. So he'd set up his old camp cot in the dining room, and by dribs and drabs the things he needed were brought down to the main floor. Vera, his cleaning lady, had helped with much of it. But Vera only came once a week. The rest of the time, Simon was enlisted for the task.

Mr. Hawkins' memory had suffered since his fall. He tended to forget things. So he kept a notepad and pencil on the table by his chair. And when Simon arrived with the dinner each day, there would be a list of things the old man had jotted down for him to fetch from the second floor.

As soon as Simon had set down the tray on the table and switched on the evening news, Mr. Hawkins would consult his list. He'd sit for a minute puzzling over his scrawl, for he had a slight tremor in his hands that wobbled his words.

"Like writing in the midst of a quake," he said.

When he managed to decipher the note, often what he'd written came as a surprise to him. "What could I have wanted *that* for?" he'd say. And then he'd remember and laugh it off, and Simon would be sent to fetch it down.

> *—two hankies from the top drawer of the tall*
> *dresser in the front room.*
> *—black belt hanging on the hook behind the*
> *closet door.*
> *—tall book with green binding on shelf below*
> *the convex mirror in the library.*
> *—section one of manuscript in the study.*

"Think of it as a bit of an adventure," he said, as if Simon were striking out on an expedition to some remote corner of the globe. And all the while he was off on his mission, the old man sat downstairs at his dinner, urging him on.

The wall by the stairs was lined with photos. There were shots of a young, tanned Mr. Hawkins on the sites of various digs. One showed him standing with a young woman at the entrance to a shaft sunk in the desert sand. There was a photo of Eleanor and him at a market stall hung with mirrors. Another, of the two of them standing on the deck of a ship, gazing out over a sea as still as glass.

"Don't linger, Simon," came the old man's voice. "Onward! Onward!"

The mirrors met him at the top of the stairs—a multitude of them, mounted everywhere on the walls. Mirrors of all shapes and sizes, from tiny pocket mirrors to tall pier glasses, some as bright and clear as crystal, others mottled and dull with age. As he moved along the dim hall, they gazed silently after him.

At one end of the hall stood a large bedroom, facing onto the street. A vanity with an oval mirror stood in the corner near the window. On the table lay a hand mirror shaped like a peacock, its long neck bent back upon itself to form the handle, its fantail flaring in a blaze of painted enamels on the mirror's back. Two dressers stood side by side against one wall. On the wall opposite, a four-poster bed with a bright coverlet into which countless tiny mirrors had been sewn. A large old leather case covered in faded travel stickers stood at its foot.

And everywhere he looked, the mirrors lurked. They merged in seamlessly with the furnishings, taking him by surprise as they peered from their places on the wall. He walked up close to stare into them. They seemed to brighten at his approach, as if they were lonely and craved reflections.

There were humble mirrors of tin that gave but the dimmest of reflections; ancient mirrors of bronze, coated in corrosion that had quenched their light. There were mirrors of burnished gold or silver, and one of black volcanic rock that held shadowy reflections in its murky depths. With so many mirrors about, he found it hard to keep his mind on his task. He fetched the hankies from the dresser, the belt from the back of the closet door.

The middle room was lined with books and mirrors from floor to ceiling. A convex mirror gaped from the wall opposite the door like a bulbous eye, swallowing the room whole in its hungry gaze. As he leaned toward it to pluck the book from the shelf below, it made his face look monstrous.

One day, Mr. Hawkins had noticed him taking an interest in the books on the shelves downstairs. "You may borrow any book you'd like," he said. "Books are like mirrors; they yearn for the company of eyes."

Books were scarce in Simon's house. So borrow he did. Hardly a day went by that he did not take one book or another down from the shelves and carry it home. There were stories of adventure and exploration, tales of far-off times and places. But his favorites by far were the books of colored engravings that stood on the bottom shelf beneath the all-seeing eye of the convex mirror. He took one out now.

"Don't forget my manuscript," came the old man's voice up the stairs.

The study stood at the rear of the second floor. A full-length mirror mounted on its door stretched the hall to twice its length. As Simon hurried now along the hall a second Simon came scurrying down the mirror hall to meet him.

The study had started out as a sunroom. Windowed on three sides, it overlooked the large wild yard. Below the windows were shelves lined with books.

A large oak desk stood in the center the room. Laid out on it in numbered sections was the manuscript of the book Mr. Hawkins had been working on in his retirement.

It was on the subject closest to his heart, the history and lore of the mirror.

Since breaking his leg, he'd been unable to get upstairs to work on it. "I feel like a squirrel in a cage down here," he said one day. "If I don't get back to work, I'll go right round the bend."

So Simon had helped clear a space at one end of the dining room table for him to work at. And now another of his tasks would be to bring down sections of the manuscript as Mr. Hawkins needed them. Today it was section one he'd been sent for. He found it on the top left corner of the desk, sitting in front of a squat computer, its screen furred with dust. Across the topmost page, under a circled number 1, the title "Soul Catchers" appeared above the text. His eyes drifted down the page, then turned to the next. Before he knew it, he was caught—as surely as the mirrors caught him if he stopped to peer in them.

"Simon, have you fallen down a crevasse up there? Are you trapped on a narrow ledge with no way to turn back? Shall I send out a rescue party?"

"Coming," he said.

Scooping up the manuscript with the rest of the things he'd been sent for, he headed back downstairs. The dinner was long since done, the television switched off. Dusk had settled like a shadowy visitor in the room.

"Ah, the wayward traveler returns," said Mr. Hawkins. "Just set those things down over there."

As he put the manuscript down on the dining room table Simon's eyes fell on the title again, and the question came tumbling out.

"Why is it called 'Soul Catchers'?" he asked.

"Ah, so that's it," said Mr. Hawkins with a smile as he switched on the lamp by his chair. "Well, long ago, people believed that when they were born, a double of themselves was born with them. They believed this double accompanied them all through life. Normally, it was hidden from sight. But if they looked in a still pool or a piece of polished metal, it was the double that looked back. For these people, their reflection wasn't just an image. It was a vital part of them—their soul, they believed. So mirrors, quite literally, were soul catchers.

"All over the world there were superstitions around mirrors and pools. People refused to look into a dark pool for fear the demon that lived there would snatch their soul and carry it under, and they would die. They believed it was bad luck, when visiting someone's house, to look in their mirror, for fear that when you left, a part of you would be left behind, in their power.

"Most of the earliest mirrors that have come down to us were tomb mirrors, buried by ancient people with their dead to catch the soul and keep it from wandering. To this day, there are people who cover the mirrors in their house after a death, in the belief that the soul of the dead person lingers there for a time and may carry off the souls of the living reflected there. So too, in times of sickness, when the soul's connection with the body is believed to be loose, people cover the mirrors in the sickroom, in case the soul of the sick person wanders off and fails to find its way back.

"Speaking of failing to find your way back, you really must hurry on home now or your mother will have my head. Start this old man talking about mirrors, and there's no end to it, I'm afraid."

As he crossed the road, Simon looked down the laneway that ran by their house and saw Dad's car parked on the weedy patch of gravel by the garage. Most of Granddad's things had been exiled to the garage—too much for the tiny house to hold, but too steeped in memory for Mom to throw out. With the garage full of Granddad's things, there was no room left for the car.

Dad started early at the butcher shop and sometimes worked too late to eat with the family. He was eating his dinner in the living room, watching the ball game on TV, when Simon came in. He sat perched over his plate, still in his work clothes, his white shirt rolled up over his muscular arms, the top two buttons undone; spots of blood on the front of his shirt, shreds of sawdust on the cuffs of his pants.

"Hey, Simon. Everything okay with Mr. Hawkins?"

"Yeah, we just got talking," said Simon. As he leaned to look at the score on the screen he caught the smell of the shop on Dad—the scent of sawdust and raw meat that worked its way into his very pores.

Simon carried the tray through to the kitchen. As he emptied the dishes into the sink, he caught sight of his face in the polished surface of the tray.

Soul catchers, he thought.

4

There were supposed to be four swings, but some yahoo had whipped two of them up over the top till they were wound tight around the crossbar, out of reach. If he'd been Supersimon, he would have shimmied up the pole and swung across to unwind them. But he wasn't—so he waited patiently in line, hanging onto Babs' hand so she wouldn't run off and lose their place.

Babs didn't like having her hand held. You could tell this right off by the way she kept squealing and tugging on his arm. The moms in line arched their eyebrows and murmured among themselves as their children stood meekly by their sides, watching the show.

He bent down and said, "Stop it right now, Babs. Do you hear me?"

"No, Dimon," she wailed. "My wan dee Mamma."

"Well you can't see Mamma. She's at work now."

Granddad's old house was proving to be a money pit. It was one thing after another. Now it looked like the furnace might need replacing. Dad was working long hours at the shop, but it still wasn't enough. To help make ends meet, Mom had taken on some hours at the Busy Bee where she'd worked as a cashier before Babs was born— which meant that Simon had to take up the slack at home, minding Babs.

"And if you don't stop your screaming, I'm going to take you home and put you to bed."

This had an instant effect. She screamed twice as loud and tried to fling herself down on the grass. The line dissolved around them as, one by one, the moms whisked their children away before they picked up any pointers from Babs. Suddenly, there were two free swings. He plunked Babs down on one. She turned off her tears like a tap.

He pushed the swing in a shallow arc and watched her waggle her toes in delight. He pushed lightly against the small of her back, and away swung all the embarrassment and anger, and the park swung open around him. And the sounds of kids whirling on the roundabout and winding down the slide were stitched in with the steady creaking of the swing.

"Push more, Dimon."

"Okay, but you hold on tight."

Someone came around behind him and settled a little boy about Babs' age onto the empty swing. Simon cringed. Babs wasn't always good with swing partners. He worried how she might react.

"No, Max, you can't have *that* swing. The little girl is using it now." It was a girl's voice, somehow familiar. "They always want the one they can't have. It's some sort of toddler law."

She seemed to be talking to him. "Oh, hi," he said, glancing over. It was the new girl at school. He couldn't come up with her name. He began trawling through the alphabet, searching for it.

She'd appeared a few days after school started up—a small, quiet girl with glasses, who looked younger than the rest of the class. She sat at the back by the door, as if she wasn't too sure she wanted to be there. He knew how that felt.

He'd seen her walking by the fence in the yard at lunch, her head buried in a book. She was a whiz at math and science, light-years beyond the rest of the class. Miss Court would call her up to the front to solve problems on the board. The other girls tittered in their seats over her frumpy clothes and funny round glasses. She didn't pay them any mind. Her head was somewhere else.

"You're Simon, right?" she said now.

"That's right." He felt his face flush. What *was* her name?

"I'm Abbey," she said. "This here is Max, my little brother. He's two. If he's lucky, he might make it to three."

While they were talking, Simon kept pushing Babs on the swing. Every time she swung past the little boy, she gave him a look.

"No," she said, just to let him know how things stood between them.

"This is Babs," said Simon. "And *that's* her favorite word."

"Hi, Babs," said Abbey. "I like your name. Max, say 'hi' to Babs."

"No," said Max.

Abbey and Simon looked at one another and laughed.

Abbey started pushing Max on the swing. If Babs swung past him, he'd say, "No." If Max swung past her, Babs would say the same. The only way to make peace was to push them at precisely the same time in exactly the same arc. It took a little doing, but Abbey was totally into it. In no time at all they'd mastered the art, and Babs and Max laughed and chattered away, while Simon and Abbey talked.

Actually, Abbey did most of the talking. She was one of those people who could talk without breathing once they got going. All he had to do was nod his head and throw in the odd question now and then.

It turned out her family had just moved to Caledon. Her dad had a job teaching at the college. There were no other kids—just Max and her. They lived in one of the big houses on the far side of the park. She was crazy smart. She'd skipped a grade and was a year younger than Simon.

She had it all figured out: what university she was going to go to, what she was going to major in, what she was going to be—a microbiologist like her dad—where she was going to live, how many kids she was going to have, and when she was going to have them. Fifteen minutes of pushing swings together in the park and he knew her whole life—even the part of it she hadn't lived yet.

"What do *you* want to be?" she asked.

He gave her a blank look. The truth was, he hadn't much thought about it. As he scrambled for an answer the swing bumped into him, throwing off the rhythm.

"Maybe a butcher," he said, for the sake of saying something.

As it turned out, it was the wrong thing. Abbey was a raging vegetarian—had been since she'd seen some documentary on TV when she was seven. *Seven*? He was watching cartoons when he was seven. Actually, he was *still* watching cartoons—with Babs, of course. Abbey had converted her entire family to vegetarianism. If there'd been more time now, she would have started in on him. But it was getting late, and once the swings went out of sync, Babs and Max began to "no" one another again.

Abbey and Simon quickly gathered up their things. They said a quick goodbye and started off in opposite directions through the park with the kids. They hadn't gone far when Abbey turned and called after him.

"Simon?"

"Yeah?"

"I forgive you."

"For what?"

"For being a carnivore."

"Okay," he said.

He looked it up when he got home.

After meeting at the swings that day, they smiled and nodded to one another in the hall at school. But he felt tongue-tied and shy with the other kids around.

As soon as the bell rang at the end of the day, she was out like a shot. Sometimes he managed to catch up to her, breathless from running, and they walked home together along the labyrinth of winding streets on the far side of the park.

They talked about this and that. She was easy to talk to.

He told her about taking dinner to Mr. Hawkins, and about the old man's mirror collection. He told her about the book on mirrors Mr. Hawkins was working on, what he'd said about mirrors being soul catchers. She was a lot smarter than he was in most things, but he knew more about mirrors.

"People used to believe that they were born double," he told her. "When they looked in a mirror, they thought it was the double that looked back."

"Wow, that's interesting, Simon," she said.

They parted in front of a large house with a pillared concrete porch with a little red wagon parked on it that must have belonged to Max. He wondered what she'd think of Granddad's tiny house.

Once hockey season started, the guys at the end of the street switched from baseball to road hockey. When they learned Simon had a net, they were more than happy to let him play. He was pretty good at hockey. He used to play with a few kids in the laneway behind the old place.

But he always knocked off early to take dinner to Mr. Hawkins. He was learning more about mirrors than he ever thought he'd know. The old man was still a little forgetful after his fall. And at times he acted like Eleanor was still around. But generally he was doing okay.

Everything was going along fine. And then one day, late in October, a letter came for Mr. Hawkins—a handwritten letter on pale blue paper, with an airmail sticker and a foreign stamp.

After that, everything changed.

5

He plucked the letter from the old man's mailbox on his way in with the dinner and put it on the tray. In the hall, he ran into Vera. She was just getting ready to leave, pulling her coat on over the pale blue smock she wore while she worked.

"Hello, Simon," she said with a wink. "What do you have for me tonight?"

Vera had been the Hawkins' cleaning lady for years. She wasn't much younger than the old man herself, and not as spry as she'd once been. But she was a habit with Mr. Hawkins and knew his ways. Every Friday, regular as clockwork, she came by to clean the floors, vacuum the rugs, and chase the dust from the furniture and the books. She kept a small transistor radio in the pocket of her smock, and an earphone in one ear, and sang to herself while she worked.

Once a month, she cleaned the mirrors. She wore cotton gloves when she did, for the mirrors were old, and a fingerprint in the wrong place could cause corrosion. She used a two-handed technique; in one hand she held a soft brush that wouldn't damage the delicate frames, while in the other she cradled the nozzle of the vacuum to suck up the dust. A soft chamois cloth was all she ever used on the glass; cleaning spray could damage the frames, or seep in behind the glass and corrode the coatings on the backs of the mirrors.

She took a peek now under the inverted plate that covered the meal Simon had brought. "My, that looks *good*," she said—just loud enough for Mr. Hawkins to hear. "Yes, *mighty* good."

"Don't you be touching that, Vera," the old man called from the front room.

She chuckled with delight and her ample body shook. She set her hat on over the wig she always wore, and headed for the door.

"You take care now, Simon," she said. "Goodbye, Mr. Hawkins."

Mr. Hawkins was sitting in his chair scratching at his leg above the cast when Simon came in.

"I'll be glad when this cursed thing is off," he said. "The itch of it's driving me mad."

"Won't be long now," said Simon, setting the tray down and wheeling the table round in front of the old man. He tried to sound cheerful, but the thought of it saddened him.

Mr. Hawkins noticed the letter on the tray. "What's this?" he said, turning it over. "Odd—no return address." He studied the postmark. "London," he said, and laid it aside.

"Anything you need me to get from upstairs?" asked Simon.

"Yes, you could fetch these books for me from the study," he said, handing Simon a slip of paper from his pad.

As Simon passed the mirrors on his way to the study, he looked at them differently than he had at first. Until recent times, mirrors were rare things, according to Mr. Hawkins. At one time, people seldom looked at themselves. And when they did, what they saw was a distorted, murky image. In those days mirrors were believed to be dangerous, almost enchanted things.

It wasn't until the development of the modern mirror with its flawless reflections that mirrors became more widespread. Even then, for a long time they were a luxury only wealthy people could afford. It wasn't till the mid-nineteenth century that mirrors became a common sight in people's homes.

Late afternoon light filled the study. A breeze blew through the open window, rustling the papers on the desk. A few had drifted to the floor. He picked them up and returned them to their piles, then went to close the window.

It was jammed. As he struggled to free it he glanced down into the yard. Mom said that when Eleanor Hawkins was alive, the wide flowerbeds that bordered the yard were full of perennials and flowering shrubs. Now they were a haven for weeds. The bushes had grown rank and tangled, their branches launching nearly as high as the tall fence that bordered the yard.

As he looked there now he was surprised to see a large dog tucked in the ragged shadows of the bushes at the back of the yard. It was a lean, hungry-looking thing, its short, dark fur almost blending in with the shadows. It rested on its belly, perfectly still, its forelegs extended in front of it, its neck and head erect, its tall pricked ears twitching like antennae as it stared up at him. Its eyes were large and knowing. Even at this distance there was something in the cold unwavering gaze it cast his way that made his skin crawl.

Suddenly, the window yielded. The sash banged down with a shiver against the sill. He looked back at the bushes, but the dog had disappeared.

He began looking for the books he'd been sent for. He ran his eyes repeatedly along the shelves, but all he kept seeing were those cold eyes. When he finally got down with the books, he found the living room empty, the food on the tray barely touched. The letter lay open by the plate.

Mr. Hawkins was in the kitchen, running water in the sink, his back to Simon. He reached up, took down a glass from the cupboard, filled it, and turned off the tap.

"You hardly touched your dinner," said Simon. "Should I leave it?"

"Yes, would you?" he said and took a long drink.

"I put those books you wanted on the dining room table."

"Fine," said the old man. He sounded strange.

Shifting the letter aside, Simon transferred the dishes to the TV table from the tray. The news was over. It was a game show now. The babble might have been in a foreign tongue. A burst of laughter sounded somehow sinister. He walked over and switched off the set. He stole a quick peek in the bronze mirror on the way back. It was utterly still. For the first time, he noticed there was an eye inscribed on its face.

He said a quick goodbye to Mr. Hawkins and headed for the door with the tray. As he crossed the street he looked back twice to make sure the dog wasn't following him.

6

One night the following week, they were in the kitchen eating dinner. Things were a little tight around the small table. Dad had gotten home early enough to eat with them, and after having spent the morning at Mrs. Pimentel's daycare for the first time, Babs had decided she was a "big girl" now and insisted on sitting at the table with everyone else. Too tired to argue, Mom stacked two phone books and an old Sears catalogue on a chair and plopped Babs down beside Simon.

At the moment, Babs was putting up a fuss because her foods were touching. As Simon carefully shepherded her peas with his fork to the far side of the plate away from her "mast 'tatoes" he was listening intently to Mom's conversation. She was telling Dad about her trip to the hospital that morning with Mr. Hawkins to have his cast removed. Things had not gone well.

"I called him yesterday to remind him I'd be coming by at ten this morning to pick him up," she said. "He sounded fine, said he couldn't wait to get the bloody thing off."

Babs looked up from her plate. She had a keen ear for curse words. "Buddy fing," she muttered, laying it down in her memory bank for future use.

"But when I called on him this morning, after dropping Babs off at Mrs. Pimentel's, he came to the door in his *pajamas*. He said he had no idea we were going to get his cast removed, swore up and down I'd never called him. I waited in the living room while he went to get dressed. He has these little notes all over the place. And right by the phone there was one reminding him I'd be taking him to the hospital this morning.

"The cab had already arrived by the time he reappeared. He'd done up the buttons on his shirt all wrong, and he was wearing his old gardening shoes, because 'someone had hidden his good shoes somewhere.' I helped him re-button his shirt; we grabbed his coat from the hall, and off we went.

"While we were waiting to see the doctor, he kept wandering off down the hall. He seemed fretful, preoccupied by something. But once we finally got in, he was all charm with the X-ray technician and the young resident that cut off the cast. Completely lucid—like you'd switched on a light in a dark room.

"The doctor took a look at the X-rays, examined his leg, and was happy with how it had healed. She gave him a walking cast to wear for a while, but he could take it off to bathe and when he went to bed. She told him to take it easy and not put any undue stress on the leg.

"On the way back he talked about how free he felt without 'that great hulking thing' on his leg. But as we neared home again he grew quiet, and there was this vagueness in his eyes when he looked at me. Twice, he called me Eleanor.

"I'm not sure what's going on, but I'm worried. I think this whole upset with the fall and the head injury took more of a toll on him than we thought. I hope that now that the cast's off, things will start to return to normal, and he'll be all right. In the meantime, it's probably best to keep bringing his dinner to him, Simon. At least then we'll know he's eating properly, and we can keep an eye on him."

Simon nodded. He too had noticed a change in Mr. Hawkins over the past week. He seemed distracted much of the time. Most nights, he didn't finish his dinner—which wasn't at all like him. And work on the book had come to a standstill.

That evening, Simon ran into Vera as she was leaving. She came out the front door as he was coming up the porch stairs with the old man's dinner. It was as if she'd been waiting for him.

"Goodbye, Mr. Hawkins," she called over her shoulder and drew the door closed behind her.

"He's not himself," she said in a low voice. "I thought he'd be happy to have that cast off. But something's troubling him. I've never seen him this way. Has anything happened recently?"

"Nothing. Well, there was a letter that came."

"What kind of letter?"

"An airmail letter. From London, he said. He didn't talk to me about it."

"Well, something's sure set him off. He's talking crazy. Say, you haven't seen any strangers around the house, have you? He's taken this notion into his head that there are prowlers on his property. He made me go around today and make sure all the downstairs windows were locked." She shook her head and started off down the stairs.

Mr. Hawkins was standing over by the dining room table when Simon came into the room with the tray. He was rifling through the papers on the table, looking for something. These days, he seemed to be constantly searching for things he'd tucked away in some strange place or other.

He looked at Simon blankly a moment, then saw the tray and, leaning on his cane, limped over to his chair in his new cast and sat down. He was wearing the clothes he'd worn to the hospital that morning, right down to his old gardening shoes.

"Switch that fool thing on for me, will you, Simon?" he said as he lifted the cover from his dinner plate.

With the newscaster droning on in the background and the dinner underway, things fell into their regular pattern. For the first time in days, Mr. Hawkins had jotted a couple of things down on his notepad, and sent Simon in search of them.

The strangeness that had come over the old man had cast its pall over all. As Simon hurried along the hall to the bedroom, the familiar creak of floorboards unnerved him.

And the shadowy reflection that gaped back at him from the vanity mirror so startled him that he gasped.

He found the sweater he'd been sent for in the dresser, and was just taking down the dusty old book on Egyptian magic from the top shelf in the library when the voice came snaking up the stairs.

"Have you found them, Davey?"

It was not the first time in recent days that the old man had called him by his granddad's name.

"Yes, I'm just coming."

"While you're up there, would you check that the windows in the study are locked? Be sure the catches are snug. I worry with that tree so close to the house. There are prowlers about."

There he was, 'talking crazy' as Vera would say. But there was something more than craziness in his tone—something that sounded unmistakably like fear.

Simon's double ran to meet him as he hurried down the hall to the study. Setting down the things he'd fetched on the desk, he went to check the windows. The wind was up, and a branch from the old tree was rapping against the glass like a bony finger.

All the windows were locked but one—the one that was often left open to air the room. Over time, the sill had swollen from being exposed to the rain and damp, and the window wouldn't close tight enough now for the lock to catch. He managed to wrestle the edge of it into place, but the slightest jolt would dislodge it. He glanced down into the yard. Again, there was no sign of the dog he'd seen that day. He'd all but convinced himself he'd imagined the whole thing.

Mr. Hawkins was back at the dining room table when Simon came into the living room. "Did you check those windows?"

"Yeah, they're all locked."

The book let out a puff of dust as he laid it on the table. There was a large stylized eye tooled in gold on the cover, like the one he'd seen inscribed on the mirror. At another time he might have asked him about it, but the old man had already opened the book and was busily searching the index for something.

Simon went to fetch the tray from the TV table. As he bent to pick it up, his eye was drawn to the mirror. The surface was in turmoil. Shadows swirled around the rim, and the surface churned. As it settled, a scene opened in the mirror.

He saw a figure running in the moonlight, clutching a mirror close to his chest—a mirror like this one, but dimmed and dark. Suddenly, at the center of it, an eye opened, as if someone had walked up out of the dark at the heart of the mirror and pressed their eye to a hole. It rested there a moment unseen by the running man. And then the rounded dome of a skull rose up from the surface of the mirror, pushing against the runner's arm, and a shadowy form flowed out and fell to the ground at his feet. Eyes wide with terror, he dropped the mirror and tore off into the night.

The tray fell with a clatter to the table. The old man looked up.

"What did you see there?"

"Nothing," lied Simon. But there *was* nothing now. The

scene had vanished, and the mirror was as it had been before. He felt dizzy, as if he'd been spun on the roundabout. He said a quick goodbye and made for the door with the tray.

Several nights over the next couple of weeks, the old man called the house, complaining of prowlers on his property. Simon watched from his bedroom window as Dad trekked across the street with a flashlight to inspect the old man's yard.

He watched the beam of light pan slowly over the dark yard, plumbing the shadows, saw Dad trudge wearily up the porch steps when he was done to rap on Mr. Hawkins' door and talk with him a minute, and then make his way back across the street, the flashlight hanging slack by his side.

"Nothing again," he said one night as Simon stood listening at the top of the stairs. "There's no one there, Jen. Those prowlers are all in his mind. But he's sure there's something out there. I can see it in his eyes."

"Oh, dear," said Mom. "What are we going to do?"

"I don't know. But if this goes on much longer, we'll have to do something."

7

The living room was the same old sickly green it had been when Granddad lived in the house. After several months of sleeping downstairs and waking to it every morning, Mom had had enough.

But now—with the floors covered in drop cloths as the painters set to work, and the furniture from the front room crammed into the hall so tight you had to squeeze past sideways to get to the kitchen, and Babs wailing because nothing was where it was "uppost" to be, and the new carpet lying propped against the porch rail outside because it had arrived a week earlier than it should have—she was going out of her mind. Simon took one look at her frazzled expression and offered to take Babs to the park.

It was the end of October. Fall had settled in, and there was a chill in the air. As he bent down to zip up Babs' sweater he glanced across at the Hawkins house. There was a bike up on the porch, padlocked to the railing. Mr. Hawkins had a visitor. Simon wondered who it could be.

There wasn't a soul in sight at the park. They shuffled through the slick leaves toward the swings. It had rained in the night, and the ruts were puddled under the swings. As he pushed Babs slowly back and forth, an upside-down Babs swung past in the puddle under her, their toes nearly touching.

He kept glancing across to the far side of the park, hoping Abbey might appear. Suddenly he heard her voice, and saw her tromping across the wet grass, pulling Max behind her in the little wagon he'd seen on the porch.

"I had a feeling you might be here," she said. "You okay, Simon? You look a little tired. Where were you yesterday?"

"I was home sick."

"You're sick a lot."

"Yeah. Some weird flu or something. Fever, chills, fatigue. I keep thinking it's over, and then suddenly it's back again." He thought back to the first time he was home with it. The day Mr. Hawkins fell from the ladder.

He wanted to tell Abbey about what he'd seen in the mirror the other day. But he couldn't think of a way of saying it that didn't make him sound crazy. If he'd known how long it would be before he'd see her again, he might have tried a little harder.

Babs and Max tried out every swing. They went on the slide countless times, with Abbey stationed at the bottom of the stairs as they climbed up, and Simon at the foot of the slide to catch them as they came down, before they landed in the puddle. At last, they were all tired and it was time to head home. Abbey gave Babs a little hug as she said goodbye, then turned and gave him one, too. He watched her shuffle off through the leaves, pulling Max behind her in the wagon.

As he was heading back home with Babs, a woman in a blue bicycle helmet cycled by on the bike he'd seen on the Hawkins porch. Their eyes met, and she bobbed her head in greeting.

The smell of paint hit him like a brick as he came through the door. He retreated upstairs. While Babs was down for her nap, he stretched out on his bed with the book of old colored prints he'd borrowed from Mr. Hawkins. One was of a square-rigged sailing ship on a raging sea in a storm. He imagined how frightened you'd be on a foundering ship in the middle of the ocean, no land in sight.

He could barely keep his eyes open. He laid his head down on the open book and dropped into a dead sleep. He found himself out on the open sea in a small boat, battered by waves as high as the house. Another passenger was in the boat with him, a shrouded woman with eyes like the eye in the mirror. She sat still as stone in the prow of the little boat as it plummeted down massive canyons of water.

When he woke up, the painters were packing up to leave. Dad had come home from work early and offered them a few extra bucks to help him haul the new carpet in off the porch and put the furniture back in place. It looked like someone else's room now, with their furniture sitting bewildered in its midst.

The smell of the fresh paint and the new carpet made him feel queasy. He was glad when it came time to take dinner across to Mr. Hawkins, so he could escape it awhile.

He brought the book back with him. The page with the ship at sea was a little damp where he'd drooled on it in his sleep.

He found Mr. Hawkins sitting at a clearing in the clutter of books and papers that covered the dining room table. Pen in hand, he was bent over some official-looking document. A small wooden box full of papers lay open beside him. A chair had been drawn up next to his, and two empty teacups sat on the table. Mr. Hawkins had shaved and changed. He seemed more like his old self than he had in weeks. Simon wondered if it had anything to do with the visitor to the house that day.

"I brought back your book," he said as he put the tray down on the TV table. It was the second time he'd borrowed it.

The old man pushed aside the papers and capped his pen. "You really like these old Currier and Ives prints, don't you?" he said. "These were the poor man's paintings, back in those days. People would buy them to hang on their walls." The loose, gummed prints fluttered like flags as he fanned through the pages. He set the open book down on the table in front of him.

He had shed his walking cast and was eager to show Simon how he could walk across the room to his armchair without his cane.

"Just a couple of books from the study on the list today," he said. He tore the top page from his notepad and handed it to Simon. "And you could take this back up. It goes in the bottom drawer of the desk in the study." He packed a few papers into the box, closed the lid, and handed it to him.

Simon breathed a sigh of relief as he headed off up-stairs. The mirrors had the bright, eager look they got when Vera dusted them. They snatched at his reflection as he hurried past.

It was warm in the sun-drenched study. When he bent to put the box back in the bottom drawer, it seemed as if the floor did a slow tilt beneath him. He felt suddenly faint. He sat down on the desk chair and waited for it to pass. There was a weird chemical taste at the back of his mouth, as if he'd been chewing carpeting and chugging it down with paint. He went to open the window, hoping the cool air might clear his head. Something tucked against the bushes at the back of the yard caught his eye. It was the dog he'd seen before. It sat in exactly the same place, in the very same stance, staring up at him.

Maybe it wasn't a dog at all, he thought. Maybe it was just one of the bushes, and it was only the distance and the play of light and shade that had turned it into a dog. Even now, he noticed a faint fluttering of the form as the breeze ruffled the leaves of the bushes around it. He began looking for the books he'd been sent for. But even as he did, a plan took shape in his mind.

When he left the house that night, he paused at the foot of the porch steps and took a quick peek back over his shoulder. He set the tray down on the edge of the steps and slipped quietly to the side of the house. Reaching his hand up through the hole in the gate, he felt for the latch and let himself into the yard.

He followed the same path he'd watched Dad take when he was searching for prowlers. He prayed the dog would have no more substance than they had. All the same, as he stole along the narrow walk he grabbed an old garden hoe he found leaning against the side of the house to arm himself against the ghost.

He tramped through the rank grass toward the rear of the yard along the trail his dad had blazed. The roses waved their long spiked branches like wands over his head. The grass had lapped up over the line of bricks that once edged the flowerbeds, so that it was hard to tell now where grass ended and flowerbed began.

Brandishing the hoe in both hands, he approached the bushes that ran across the back of the yard. They launched themselves high and wild, weaving their straggly branches together, so that the fence behind was all but hidden by them.

His hands gripped the hoe so hard they hurt. He wondered how quickly he could tear back through the overgrown grass to the safety of the street should the dog appear. He plumbed the shadows behind the bushes, but there was nothing there. He reached out cautiously with the hoe and lifted the low sweeping branches under a couple of the bushes. Still there was nothing.

Glancing back at the study windows, he gauged as well as he could where it was he'd seen the dog sitting. The grass behind him lay trodden flat where he'd walked. Yet at the spot near the bushes, where the dog had been, it stood erect and undisturbed. He reached out and parted it with the hoe to see if anything might support what he'd seen—prints in the soil, a tuft of fur. But there was nothing.

Here the bushes were particularly thick. Some varieties were more vigorous than others. One smaller bush with dark umber leaves had been so blocked out by the larger bushes that grew to either side of it that it had launched its branches out low over the grass.

Maybe this was what he'd seen from the study window—this narrow wedge of dark between the larger bushes. A flutter of wind had woken it to life, and imagination had opened a pair of chill eyes in the illusion. He reached out with the hoe to poke the bush—and heard a sound that made his blood run cold.

It was a growl, the low, threatening growl of a dog that had been disturbed. He stepped back slowly, peering into the shadows. There was not a sign of movement. Nothing. It was just the groan of branches grating against one another when he disturbed them with the hoe, he told himself.

And then he heard it again—a deep guttural growl, louder this time, accompanied by a furtive movement from somewhere deep in the shadows of the bushes. And then, at the heart of the leaves, there was a glimmer as two cold eyes glared back at his.

He turned and tore from the yard, dropping the hoe behind him in the grass. He ran for his life, not once daring to look back. Racing across the street, he dashed breathless into the house.

"What is it, Simon?" said Dad. "You look like you've seen a ghost."

"It's nothing," he said.

And when Mom asked what happened to the tray, he said he'd forgotten it and would get it in the morning. One thing he knew for sure, there was no way he was going back to fetch it now.

The smell of paint and carpet hung like a toxic fog in the air. No one else seemed bothered by it, but his head reeled from the reek of it.

After dinner, he crept off to his room. He sat at his window, sucking in the cool air, staring across at the Hawkins house as the dark came down and settled over the yard and its terrors, and the lights winked on in the downstairs room where the old man cocked his ear for prowlers.

The tray sat on the porch steps where he had left it. By and by, the shadows deepened till he could see it no more.

8

He woke with a start to the sound of Mom calling up the stairs to say he'd better get moving or he'd be late for school. He had no idea what time it was, what *day* it was. When he sat up, the room began to spin. He was so exhausted he could hardly pull his clothes on.

It had taken him ages to fall asleep. And when he finally did drop off, he found himself right back in the Hawkins yard. Again, he heard the chill growl from the bushes. Only now it seemed something more than a growl, and the eyes that looked back at him through the leaves were level with his own. He woke in a sweat, heart pounding, and lay wide-eyed in the dark listening to a dull, rumbling throb pulsing from a car outside.

He looked out the window now and saw the tray still sitting on the steps. The trip across the street to retrieve it left him limp and breathless.

"You look awful, Simon," said Mom as he set the tray down on the counter. "Are you not feeling well again?" She put her hand to his forehead. "You've got a fever. Get right back up to bed, and I'll call the school. What *is* this thing?"

For the next couple of nights, Mom carried the dinner across to Mr. Hawkins. She was relieved to find him looking better, and said he was asking after his helper. On Wednesday, she handed Simon a note from him, along with the book of Currier and Ives prints.

Dear Simon, read the note, *I'm sorry you're not feeling well. Please accept this book as a get-well present from me. When you're well enough to come by, I have something important to tell you.*

It was the mystery as much as anything that drew Simon from the refuge of his room and sent him walking across the street to bring the old man his dinner that Friday.

Mr. Hawkins was expecting him. Simon found him sitting at the dining room table. He had shifted his books and papers to one side to make space for the tray. Centered on the table before him lay the bronze mirror. Simon stopped in his tracks.

"Just set that down here," said the old man. Then he motioned for Simon to sit down in the chair opposite him across the table, the mirror between them.

"So you got my note," he said as he uncovered the dinner plate. "And you're no doubt wondering what on earth I might have to tell you that could be so important. It concerns this mirror," he said, with a nod in its direction. "It was a favorite of Eleanor's, and I've noticed you're drawn to it, too. There's a curious story around how we happened to come by it. I find I must tell you that story now." He took a forkful of his dinner and stared down at the mirror, as if searching for where to start.

"A few years back," he began, "I was invited to speak at the annual conference of the British Archaeological Society in London. I had recently been involved in the excavation of an Iron Age cemetery in East Yorkshire, and the rich trove of artifacts we found there, including an ornate iron mirror, was to form the focus of my talk.

"Eleanor accompanied me. We stayed at a hotel where we'd often stayed years before, and planned to visit some favorite haunts and look up some old friends while we were in town.

"There was a buzz in the air about the Yorkshire find, and the talk was well-attended. As I was delivering it, I found my eye drawn more than once to a fellow who sat near the front. He stood out from the sedate, rather dusty-looking group one normally finds at such gatherings, and I wondered what had brought him there. At the reception after the talk, I was speaking to some colleagues when I noticed the same man talking to Eleanor. A few minutes later, she came up to me with him in tow.

"'Randall, I'd like you to meet Henry Winstanley,' she said. 'Mr. Winstanley is a dealer in antiques. He shares our interest in mirrors, and has put together what sounds like a very interesting collection. Recently, he acquired an item he believes we may be interested in.' And she gave me a look.

"I knew that look, just as I knew the unmistakable tone in her voice. It meant she had decided there was something here worth pursuing, and I was to stand up and take note. Eleanor had a remarkably keen eye and an astute business sense. Over the years, I'd come to trust her intuition in such matters, and more often than not it had proved correct.

"We agreed to meet with the dealer. He would show us his collection and present the item he had spoken to Eleanor about. He wasn't prepared to say anything more about it just then. He seemed strangely guarded and ill at ease, and I couldn't think why.

"Nothing more was said of the matter. Over the next few days we went about our business, and it quite went out of my mind. On our last night, I was ready to settle down to a quiet dinner, when Eleanor reminded me of our meeting with Winstanley. It was the last thing in the world I wanted to do, and I was all for cancelling. But she wouldn't hear of it. She said it wasn't far, and suggested we go on foot. She would bring along her map and be our guide.

"Our path led us far from the busy thoroughfares of the city into a labyrinth of narrow streets untouched by time. Our footsteps rang on the cobbled streets, and for the first time on our trip I felt we had recaptured something of the charm and excitement of the city we had known in our youth.

"The shop, when we came upon it at last, was one of a dozen on a dark, silent street. The others had closed their doors for the night, but *H. Winstanley—Antiques and Curios* still had a light burning inside.

"The bell chimed as we entered, but Winstanley was nowhere in sight, and we were at our leisure to look around on our own. The small shop was full of fine antique furniture, exquisite porcelains, and delicate crystal. But repeated ringings of the bell on the counter failed to rouse the owner. Eleanor was writing a note to Winstanley, explaining that we had called and failed to find him in—when there came a sudden flurry of footsteps. And out through a curtain at the rear of the shop burst Winstanley. He was wearing an apron.

"'Forgive me,' he said. 'I was upstairs preparing something for us to eat, and completely lost track of the time. I hope you haven't been waiting long.'

"Out through the curtain with him had drifted the most delicious smell. I was solidly hooked. He led us to the rear of the shop and through the curtain. Here there were even finer things than at the front of the shop. Most of his clients, he explained, were private collectors. He was their eyes and ears on the art world. He knew the sort of things they were interested in. These items had been purchased for them.

"He led us up a narrow staircase to his flat, a simple set of rooms decorated with impeccable taste. As it turned out, he *did* know a great deal about mirrors and had several fine eighteenth century French mirrors on his walls.

"The dinner was delicious. Afterward, we settled in the living room to talk. All was politeness, but there was still no sign of the mirror that had brought us there. It was growing late, and the prospect of rising early the next morning to catch our flight home had begun to weigh upon me.

"Winstanley wandered off, as I supposed, to fetch coffee. But when he returned, he was carrying an object wrapped in a piece of velvet. He set it down on the table between us and quietly uncovered it. And so it was we had our first glimpse of the Egyptian mirror. It was an impressive piece, lying there couched on its bed of velvet, and as Eleanor and I leaned down to look at it, Winstanley started in on his tale.

"'Some months back, I was at an auction here in London. A wealthy collector had recently died, and his estate was up for auction. An item one of my clients was interested in was on the block, and I was determined to carry it off for him.

"'While I was waiting, I browsed through the catalogue. Near the back, I came upon a curious item that piqued my interest. It was described as an ancient bronze Egyptian mirror. It had first surfaced in the late nineteenth century and had since passed through several hands before being acquired by its current owner. One of these was the famous clairvoyant Edward Cardwell, who had claimed it possessed magical powers.

"'It was a curiosity, and it was a mirror, so I was drawn to it. It was arcane enough that I didn't expect it would attract much interest. By the time it came up for bid, all the high rollers had long departed, and I was able to buy it for a reasonable price. It's a little outside my own area of expertise, and when I read that you would be speaking in London, I thought perhaps you might be interested in it.'

"I examined the mirror. It was a pretty thing, and possessed some interesting features. The handle, a representation of the Egyptian goddess Beset, was finely worked. There was a curious motif of intertwining snakes incised around the rim, and an eye inscribed on the face. It had all the earmarks of an Egyptian piece from the late Middle Kingdom. Yet it was clearly a fake.

"No ancient bronze mirror could possibly have been preserved as this one was. There was not a trace of patina on it, not a hint of corrosion of any kind. It was fine work by a skilled metalworker with an intimate knowledge of the production techniques of the period. But it was, at best, two or three hundred years old.

"Yet Eleanor had taken a fancy to it. It had clearly kindled something in her. Whether she believed it possessed magical powers, I didn't know. What I did know was that she had fastened upon it, and there would be no swaying her.

"I asked Winstanley what he wanted for it. He quoted a figure lower than I would have expected, and left us to mull it over while he went to make coffee. Over our years of collecting, Eleanor and I had developed a certain technique. I would seek out the initial price the dealer had in mind, and then I would leave her to bargain it down. Our collection owed much to her skill in such matters.

"So when Winstanley returned with the coffee, I made myself scarce for a time, examining his collection more closely while she worked her magic. When I got back, she gave me a sly wink. I found she had worked him down to a ridiculously low figure, less than half what he'd originally been asking. I was stunned.

"In a matter of minutes the deal was finalized. It was late when we left. As we threaded our way back through the dark, echoing streets, I had the feeling we had as good as stolen it from under his nose.

"When we got back to Caledon I consulted my friend Joan Cameron, a curator in the Egyptian department at the museum. She agreed that the mirror was a remarkably fine piece of work. She thought the Beset figure that formed the handle was especially well executed and was intrigued by the curious design around the rim and by the eye of Horus on the face of the mirror. But she echoed my opinion that it was undoubtedly a forgery.

"Eleanor was unmoved. She hung the mirror on the wall opposite her chair, and I went back to work on the book. Life settled into its normal course, and I put the whole affair out of my mind.

"Then, one day I walked into the room with our tea and found Eleanor standing staring at the mirror. She was holding the newspaper in her hand, as if she'd been about to sit down with it and had been stopped in mid-course by something she saw there. Utterly oblivious of me, she continued to stare silently, as if in a trance. I had to call her several times before she heard me.

"'Do you see that?' she asked then, still staring into the mirror.

"I went and stood behind her. 'See what?' I asked, for I could see nothing but the muted reflection of the room.

"'The image of our backyard,' she said. 'And there, that figure, peering from the bushes.' I assured her I could see nothing.

"In a matter of minutes the vision had passed, and she was her old self again.

"But it was as if a door opened in our lives that day, and afterwards things were never quite the same. Many a time I would find her standing entranced before the mirror as I had found her that day, staring into its depths at something she alone could see.

"She was able to recount quite lucidly what it was she had seen, how it had come and gone. She said that at first a ripple would run through the reflection in the mirror, and it would cloud up in the way the water in a pond does if disturbed. As it cleared, she would find some scene spread before her. There was never any sound, never any sense that she herself was part of what she saw—merely that she was observing it. Soon it would start to fade, and the mirror would return to normal.

"She interpreted what she saw as a premonition of things to come. Often it had to do with her garden, fallen into neglect, harboring some half-seen presence. It was all a fantasy, I believed, and I was all for taking it down. But she wouldn't hear of it.

"Then two years ago she suffered a heart attack in her sleep and died. It feels like yesterday. Her scent still lingers in the room. Her voice echoes down the stairs. I hear a noise and swear it's her coming down the hall. I turn and see her sitting in her chair.

"I tried taking the mirror down after she died, but it wasn't long before it found its way back up onto the wall again. It seemed to belong there. From time to time, I'd find myself standing in front of it, straining to see more than the dim reflection it cast back at me. But it was all in vain. It was never more than an ordinary mirror for me.

"And so things might have stayed were it not for that fall from the ladder that brought you here. The moment I saw you it was as if I were looking at your granddad as a boy. And some wonder woke in me again. Then one day I saw you standing in front of the mirror all still and entranced, exactly as Eleanor used to stand, and I knew that you, too, saw."

All this time the mirror lay on the table between them. Now Mr. Hawkins picked it up and returned it to its place on the wall. When he got back he began rummaging through the papers on the table, looking for something.

"Some weeks back," he said, "I received a letter from Henry Winstanley. What he had to say shook me to the core, and I'm afraid I haven't quite been myself since. Though the mirror is closed to me, I know from how it has opened to Eleanor and to you that it possesses a power. I know enough of power to know that it can be used for good or ill. If the mirror falls into the wrong hands, I fear it may be for ill. I can't allow that to happen.

"Ah, here it is," he said, plucking a letter from the pile. "Perhaps when you read this, it may help convince you that I'm not just a crazy old man." He handed the letter to Simon, who recognized it at once.

"Take it with you," said Mr. Hawkins. "It's late, and I've kept you far too long. You'd best hurry along home. The wind is up. There's a storm coming on."

9

The sky was dark and ominous. As if sensing the on-coming storm, Babs was more restless than usual. Simon could hear the light rhythmic rocking of her crib through the wall. Outside, the clouds roiled, the thunder rumbled and boomed. In the distance, lightning flashed. The rising wind shivered the streetlights on their stands and whipped the tree branches into a frenzy. Suddenly the sky opened, and the rain teemed down.

He sat by the window, watching the storm. The letter lay open on his lap. He had read it through twice, first in disbelief, then with mounting dread. In it, Winstanley confessed that when he told the Hawkinses how he'd come by the mirror, he hadn't told the whole story. It seemed there'd been someone else at the auction that day with an interest in the mirror—a woman.

He'd first caught sight of her at the viewing, before the auction began, as prospective buyers were taking a closer look at the items up for bid.

I discovered the mirror off in a corner, he wrote, *sitting on a table with a number of other small items. It had taken me some time to find it. No one else in the room had taken the trouble, and I found myself quite alone with it. It was a pretty thing—very finely crafted. I had never seen anything quite like it. It had a strangely primitive air about it.*

While I was admiring it, I noticed that a woman had detached herself from the crowd and was drifting my way. She was like a figure from another time—tall and thin, with an old-fashioned air of elegance about her. She wore a hat with a broad sweeping brim that cast her face in shadow. Most of her skin was covered—down to the long kid gloves she wore—and what was not covered was strikingly pale.

I could see little of her face save for her lips and chin. As she neared I noticed that those lips were red and full, and I realized with something of a shock that she was much younger than I'd imagined.

As she moved slowly along the line of tables I knew with some sure instinct that she would stop at the mirror. And stop she did. We stood opposite one another across the table, but not once did her gaze rise to meet mine. Her eyes were only for the mirror. She reached out and touched it, ran her gloved fingers lightly over the figure that formed the handle, with a strange familiarity. I expected an attendant to come rushing over, but no one seemed to notice.

She bent low and hovered over it, so that her face cast a murky reflection in the polished metal. She said nothing, but I heard a long low intake of breath, as though she was caught in the grip of some overpowering emotion. I felt ill at ease, as if I were intruding on some private tryst, and I retreated to my seat. When I glanced back at the table, she had gone.

The auction was called to order. As those in attendance took their seats I scanned the crowd for the mysterious woman, but she was nowhere to be seen. It quickly became apparent, once things were underway, that there was money in the room. Bids leapt to alarming heights from the start.

The Chippendale piece that had brought me to the auction went for twice the top bid my client had been prepared to make. And I was sure the mirror would be caught up in the frenzy and carried far beyond my reach.

But, once the major items had been sold, the money started to move from the room, and with it the crowd that followed in its wake. So when at last item #182: "an ancient bronze Egyptian mirror" came up, there were no more than two-dozen people left in the room.

The assistant brought the item up and displayed it to the room while the auctioneer solicited the initial bids. The little mirror did not present

well, and the auctioneer was clearly less than en-
thused by it, and eager to hurry the proceedings
along. The bidding started low and stayed there. I
topped one or two halfhearted bids, and the auc-
tioneer was about to bring the gavel down, when
he noticed a higher bid from the back of the room.

I glanced back and saw that the woman I had
seen earlier had reappeared. It was she who had
made the bid. She sat off to the side a couple of
rows behind me. For the first time, I had a clear
view of her. She was quite striking in profile, with
a proud aquiline nose, large dark eyes, and a full
mouth. She had but one flaw I could see—a scar
set high on one cheek just below the eye. I took her
to be about forty, but in truth she was ageless. I
wondered what her interest in this little mirror
could possibly be.

Beside her sat a gentleman. He was lean and
sinewy, with large questing eyes. They seemed an
unlikely couple. There was something feral in the
way he fawned upon her, constantly turning to her
to see what he should do next.

It was he who made the bids for her—with a brief
bob of his long narrow head. She looked straight
ahead, never once deigning to glance in my direc-
tion. She might have been the only one in the room.

I topped her bid, and she bettered mine. I soon
surpassed what I'd been prepared to bid for the
mirror, and began to dip into the funds my collec-
tor had put at my disposal. If I'd had any sense at

all, I would simply have let it go. But there was something in the mystery surrounding it, something in the chill allure of this woman, that drew me into danger. I suspected there was much more to her interest in the mirror than anyone in the room realized.

Before I was fully aware of it, I was drawn out far beyond my depth. When the gavel finally came down, it was like a crash of thunder that wakes one from a dream. And I found myself in possession of the mirror.

I had a sick feeling in the pit of my stomach. I wanted to shout out that there had been some mistake. The woman rose with her companion. For the first time, she turned and fixed me in her gaze. Her face was set like stone, and the look in her eyes froze me to the bone.

I carried the mirror back home with me. I tried in vain to interest my collector in it. I was seriously out of pocket and had to borrow money against the business to repay him. But in the weeks that followed, the business suddenly foundered. I was at my wits' end with worry.

Then the phone calls started coming, always late at night, shortly after I had turned out the light. There was never any reply when I picked up the phone, only the sure sense of a presence, utterly silent yet palpably malevolent, on the other end.

Night after night my sleep was troubled by the same vivid dream. I was walking through a wood and had lost my way. I was carrying the mirror with me. Behind me, I could hear some creature crashing through the undergrowth toward me. I would wake in a cold sweat. The dream began to creep into my waking life. Several times, while walking home at night along the dark streets, I heard the sound of something following me. Once, after racing back to the shop and bolting the door, I caught a glimpse of what looked like a large dog passing, a dog unlike any I had ever seen.

Soon, I refused to leave the shop for any reason after nightfall. I consulted a doctor. He diagnosed a nervous disorder, prescribed a mild sedative, and advised complete rest. I was convinced that everything that had happened since I came into possession of the mirror could be laid at its door, and I desperately wanted rid of it.

It was then I happened upon a notice of your upcoming talk at the Archaeological Society conference. I knew of your interest in mirrors, and I decided to approach you, in the hope that you might somehow be induced to buy it. I cared little what I got for it; I only wanted it gone.

I attended the conference and introduced myself to your wife. I told her of the mirror, and arranged for the two of you to come and inspect it. I could sense that you were skeptical, but I lowered the price enough that you were willing to buy it.

By the following morning you were away with it on a plane—and there was an ocean of oblivion between us. The nightmares that had plagued my sleep stopped. The presence that dogged my steps in the dark vanished like a mist, and my nervous condition with it. I was as one reborn. My business soon recovered, and all was well with the world.

I confess, to my shame, that I spared not a thought for the two of you. You belonged to a period of dark on which I had turned the page, shadows from a past I had put behind me. A while back, I learned from a colleague in the mirror world that your wife had died, and I was filled with remorse for any part I may have played in it. I am an ill man now. While once I was able to shut away the past, I am swept up in the tide of it now, and spirits are my constant companions. I relive those days repeatedly. I stand again in that auction room with the mirror lying on the table before me, and I watch that strange woman reach her lean hand down and run her fingers along it.

I have sold off my mirror collection. I can no longer bear to look at my reflection in the glass for fear of what gaunt creature I may glimpse lurking just behind me there.

Now it is done. I have said what I should have said long ago. Perhaps you will read this and wonder what madness has come upon this poor man. Perhaps the ocean between us was broad enough that this darkness could not leap it, and you have lived your lives in peace. I pray it be so.

But if darkness has somehow found its way to your door, know that it did to mine as well. Beware a woman with a scar upon her cheek, and a beast that prowls by night. I don't know why she seeks the mirror, but seek it she will—with all her passion and to your ill.

Henry Winstanley

Simon sat at the window with the letter on his lap. Waves of unreality washed over him as, outside, the torrential rain washed over all. The trees flailed to and fro. Rainwater sluiced down the street, overflowing the storm drains, pooling at the foot of the hill. It swallowed the sidewalks whole, lapped against the grass.

The Hawkins house was obscured in the downpour, cocooned with its feeble light amidst the raging storm. Simon's eyes grew heavy from squinting through the curtains of rain at it, as if watching would somehow keep it safe. Then the light in the downstairs room winked out, and there was only the wind and the rain and the all-encompassing night. He fell asleep where he sat, bundled in blankets, the rain drumming with ghost fingers against the glass.

10

He woke to the sound of Babs crying in her crib. He was lying on the floor by the window, wound in his sheet like a mummy. His feet were cold and wet. He looked down and found them resting in a puddle, where the rain had found a way in. The letter was pinned under them. Untangling himself from the sheet, he snatched it out and carefully separated the pages, draping them over the headboard of his bed.

As he sopped up the puddle with his wet pajamas he looked out the window. He half-expected to find the world submerged, the water lapping lazily against the sill, the Hawkins house up and floated away.

But there it stood, whole and still in the sunlight. The road was strewn with leaves and puddles. The trees, stripped of their leaves, stood skeletal and bare. Down the street, a large tree limb had come down in the storm and lay across the road. A car bumped up onto the sidewalk to get by.

Having failed to attract attention, Babs amped up her crying a little. Simon padded down the hall to her room and found her standing in the crib, one leg hoisted up onto the rail. It was her latest trick. She knew she wasn't supposed to do it, and she gave him an impish grin as he came into the room.

"No, Babs," he said. "Put your leg down."

It was a short step from hoisting her leg up onto the rail to launching herself right over the top. Dad had lowered the mattress as far as it would go and banished the large stuffed bear she'd boosted herself up on to the closet. But she was still managing to get that leg up.

She gave Simon a long, steady look, then slid her leg off the rail and plopped down in the crib. Her diaper and sleeper were soaked. Fragments of dream flashed into his mind as he lifted her out and laid her on the change table. He changed her diaper and dressed her and they headed downstairs.

Mom was in the kitchen, listening to the post-storm report on the radio as she prepared that night's dinner. She was working the afternoon shift at the Busy Bee, and would reheat it when she got home.

"Did the storm keep you awake last night?" she said as she grated lemon rind and knocked it into a bowl of batter.

"A little. Some water got in through the window. I wiped it up." He plopped Babs down on her chair.

"Appa do," she said. He filled her sippy cup with apple juice and handed it to her. "Cor fay," she said. He poured corn flakes into her bowl and set it down in front of her.

"They say a tornado touched down north of the city," said Mom. "A lot of damage done, but, thankfully, no one was hurt. Wilma across the street phoned to see if we had power. She doesn't. I wondered if Mr. Hawkins' power was out. I tried calling, but his phone doesn't seem to be working.

If I don't get through before I leave, maybe you could try in a while—just to make sure everything's all right. I'm making lemon pudding cake for dessert. It's his favorite."

Soon the house was full of the delicious aroma of lemon pudding cake baking. Lemma puddy cay, Babs called it—and kept calling it now until it was out of the oven and cool enough for Mom to give her a small bowlful.

"Oh, look at the time," she said and tore off to change into her uniform. Normally now, on the days she was working the afternoon shift, Mom would take Babs across to Mrs. Pimentel's. But since it was a Saturday, Simon had been enlisted for the job of giving her lunch and putting her down for her afternoon nap.

As she put on her coat Mom reminded Simon to give Mr. Hawkins a call. She gave them both a quick kiss and hurried out the door.

Babs was down to one nap a day now. She took it right after her lunch. It was as much for Mom's sake as for Babs'. This was the time she sat down with a quiet cup of tea, put her feet up on the stool, and watched her soaps. She'd usually snooze a little herself. If it was up to her, Babs would *never* drop that afternoon nap.

As it was now, Babs usually didn't need much persuading to go down. Today, after making short work of the grilled cheese sandwich Simon had made for her and cut into triangles—if it wasn't cut into triangles, she wouldn't touch it—she started getting drowsy over her second bowl of lemma puddy cay.

Babs was a creature of extremes: one minute so full of energy you swore she'd never stop, and the next, nodding off. She sat there now with her spoon clutched in her fist, staring at him glassy-eyed. Her eyelids fluttered closed and her head bobbed. At the bottom of the bob she jerked and woke herself up, and the cycle started all over again.

Simon grabbed a damp cloth and quickly cleaned her up. Speed was essential at this point. If you missed the narrow window when sleep came over her, she'd get over-tired and refuse to go down. He undid her bib and carried her up to her room, laid her down and covered her up. She tucked her thumb in her mouth and was out like a light.

Ten minutes later, as if on cue, a crew of city workers came rumbling down the street in an open truck with a chipper hitched to the back, and started in with their chainsaws, cutting up the large branch blocking the road. Simon watched from the window in his room as they cut it into logs and hoisted them onto the truck. They fed the smaller stuff into the chipper, which gobbled it up noisily and spewed chips into the back of the truck.

The floor under the window was damp, and the knees of Simon's pants were wet from kneeling there now. He kept looking over at the Hawkins house for some sign of life. But there was nothing. The weekend paper flapped in the breeze on the porch. The wind chime chattered to it-self. The dahlias hung their heads in the long grass, look-ing as if they'd never get up.

Something was wrong. He tried phoning, but the line was still dead. He watched as the work crew finished up and loaded their gear into the back of the truck. They drove off down the street, leaving scattered bits of branch and leaf on the road to tell the tale.

A knot of dread had settled in the pit of his stomach. He tried the number again. This time he got a ring, but his relief faded as the phone rang on and on. He was about to hang up when it clicked over to the answering machine. He pictured it perched by the phone in the front room.

Mr. Hawkins had told him that after Eleanor died, he somehow couldn't bring himself to erase her greeting from the machine. He said there were times he would sit and play it over and over, just to hear the sound of her voice again.

Her voice came on the line now, hauntingly strange, like someone speaking from beyond the grave. "Hello," she said. "You have reached the Hawkins residence. I'm afraid we aren't able to take your call right now. Please leave your name and number and a brief message, and we'll get back to you as soon as we can." There was a brief pause, followed by a long beep.

"Hello, Mr. Hawkins," he said. "This is Simon calling. We were wondering if you have power in your house after the storm, and if you're all right. If you can hear me, please pick up. My mom's a little worried about—" But the time was up, and the machine clicked off.

He could hear Babs talking through the wall. He hung up the phone and went to get her. She was sitting in the crib, deep in conversation with her stuffed animals. She was telling them all about the lemma puddy cay. As he lifted her out she grabbed her blue bunny by the ear and brought him along.

He settled the two of them at the kitchen table and gave Babs the bowl she'd left unfinished at lunch. She tried to give the bunny a taste, but he refused to open his stitched-on mouth to try it.

Simon wandered into the front room and looked out the window at the Hawkins house again. There was a light on now in the living room.

He felt a great weight fall from his chest. Hurrying to the kitchen, he filled a small bowl with lemon pudding cake and plucked Babs from her chair. In moments, they were out the door.

The air was fresh and pure, as though the world had been reborn. But as he crossed the street with Babs on his hip and the bowl of lemon pudding cake in his hand, the puddles in the road were dark pools into which he dared not look.

The newspaper gibbered in the wind as they came up the stairs. He set the bowl down on the wicker table and rang the bell. While he waited for Mr. Hawkins to answer the door, he glanced up at the fanlight and saw that the hall light was on as well. He cranked the bell again.

"Puddy cay," said Babs, taking his chin in her hand and turning his head till he was looking at her. He noticed that the next-door neighbor's porch light was on.

He turned and looked the other way. Two doors down, another porch light was on. His heart sank as the truth dawned on him. The power *had* been out and had just come back on. That was why the porch lights were all suddenly on. They'd been on when the power went off last night, and now when it came back on, so did they.

"Dow," said Babs, squirming in his arms till he put her down. She made a beeline for the bowl of lemon pudding cake and plopped down on the porch floor with it. She dipped her fingers in the bowl and looked up guiltily as he approached.

But Simon didn't notice her. He leaned over the table and squinted through the sheers into the front room. The floor lamp was on. Mr. Hawkins was sitting in his chair. All Simon could see of him was an elbow resting on the arm, a foot extending beyond the skirt of the chair. He rapped on the glass, but the old man didn't stir.

Then he noticed a faint trail of dirty footprints leading from the doorway of the room to the chair. Dried mud clung to the side of the old man's shoe. He knocked till his knuckles ached, but nothing moved. It was like a tableau of the room, a carefully constructed display shielded behind a barrier of glass. Only one thing was missing. The Egyptian mirror had vanished from the wall.

Babs was busy licking the inside of the empty bowl by the time he turned from the window. He scooped her up and carried her back across the street in a daze. His haunted face peered up from every puddle they passed.

They were sitting in the living room with the TV on when Mom got home. Babs was a sticky mess from the lemon pudding cake. An hour had passed, but part of him was still beating on the window of the Hawkins house.

Mom picked up Babs, then reached down and switched off the TV. She stood over him, her face full of concern.

"What's wrong, Simon?" she said.

He kept staring at the dark screen. She dropped down on her haunches in front of him and stared him straight in the face.

"What happened, Simon? Why are you like this?"

"It's Mr. Hawkins," he said, but he couldn't bring himself to say more.

PART II

STRICKEN

People believed that the souls of the sick were loose
and could easily wander off. The mirror in the sickroom was covered, lest the soul of the sick person
take flight and fail to find its way back.

-Randall Hawkins, *Soul Catchers*

11

Simon took another sip of ginger ale from the plastic cup. It was warm and flat and sticky-sweet, but it gave him something to do. Across the room, Mom and Dad were making small talk with the neighbors and friends who had come. Vera was there, along with the Glovers, the Pimentels, Mrs. Logan the cat lady, and old Miss Walker next door. It was strange to see them together in the same room.

On the far side of the room, there was a woman he'd seen before, but couldn't place. She stood out in the sparse group that had turned out for the memorial, and he found his gaze kept drifting her way. She was tall and solidly built. Her hair, threaded with grey, was drawn back in a loose bun.

She stood looking at the board of photos Mom had managed to cobble together from Granddad's pictures. The Hawkins' albums were sealed in the house, along with everything else, while the search went on for the old man's will. In the absence of a will, and with no known next of kin, the funeral had been delayed for weeks.

Simon stood near the door in his stiff Sunday clothes, beside a table where coffee, tea, and soft drinks had been set out alongside plates of cut sandwiches and store-bought cookies. Now and then a woman in a pin-stripe jacket would creep up behind him over the plush carpeting to replenish the plates. Occasionally, a lost mourner would poke their head in at the doorway, realize they were in the wrong place, and drift off down the hall to the next sad room.

He took another swallow of the warm ginger ale. He was not feeling at all well. Part of it was the place: the awful hush that hung in the air, the rank scent of cut flowers. Part of it was the clothes: the tie too tight about his throat, the woolen jacket and pants so hot he thought he might faint.

But it was more than that. Something strange and frightening was happening to him. Great waves of dizziness kept washing over him. He was barely over one when he sensed the next starting up like a faint swell on the horizon. He could feel it surging as it neared, and tried to brace himself against it before it flooded over him. But nothing seemed to help. Each wave left him feeling more battered and drained than the one before, and full of helpless dread as the next began its slow crawl toward him.

There was something terribly wrong with him, and he didn't know what it was. He hadn't felt right for a while. Several times that fall, he'd been home sick from school with fevers and chills. But he could pinpoint to the day when the sickness had hit him in earnest. The day the living room had been repainted and the new carpet laid.

The smell had made him queasy, and there'd been a weird chemical taste at the back of his mouth. The next morning, he'd woken up feeling dizzy and nauseous, so tired he could barely get out of bed.

But in the dark weeks since Mr. Hawkins died, it had grown much worse. Mom and Dad put it down to a reaction to the old man's death. But it was far more than that. It was as though the earth had opened under him and sent him hurtling into an abyss.

Another wave hit him now, rocking him on his feet. He reached out and gripped the edge of the table so hard his knuckles turned white. The room spun and his stomach pitched as some vast malevolence took and shook him till he went as limp as one of Babs' rag dolls.

He felt a sudden dampness down his leg. He looked down dully and saw that he'd crushed the plastic cup he was holding, draining its contents down the leg of his pants and onto the carpet. He felt far too unsteady on his feet to stoop down to clean up the mess. Glancing across the room to see if anyone had noticed the accident, he saw the woman at the picture board staring back. She began walking briskly in his direction.

"Damn fool things, these flimsy cups," she said as she came up to him. She urged the shattered cup from his clenched hand and dropped it into the wastebasket, scooped up a handful of napkins from the table and blotted the spill on the carpet.

"I'm Joan Cameron," she said. "And you're Simon, aren't you? I passed you on my bike one day when I was leaving Hawkins' house."

So that's who she was—Mr. Hawkins' friend from the museum. The one he'd shown the mirror to after he bought it.

"Hawkins thought the world of you," she said. "Went on about what a fine lad you were, and what a help you'd been to him since his fall. Shall we sit down?" She steered him over to a chair and handed him some napkins to dry his pant leg.

"I hate these things. Always have to force myself to come. Still, it's the least one can do for an old friend. It's a terrible shame. I was speaking to him just a few days before he died. He seemed right enough—except for this notion he'd gotten into his head that there were prowlers on his property. He was convinced someone was after that Egyptian mirror of his, though heaven knows why. We both agreed it was a fake.

"He said he'd decided that the only way to keep it safe was to hide it. Well, he must have hidden it pretty well because the trustee couldn't find a trace of it when he searched the house for the will."

"Hidden it?" said Simon, stunned. He'd never even considered the possibility. On that terrible day he found the old man dead and saw the wall empty where the mirror had hung, he'd presumed it had been taken by the woman Winstanley had warned him about in his letter. But what if it hadn't? What it he'd hidden it?

He had the strangely disembodied feeling one has when waking from a dream. He felt like he might faint. He had to get some air.

"Excuse me," he said, and stood up.

But before he could stir from the spot, another wave of dizziness struck him full on, rocking him on his feet. He saw Mom look over in alarm.

The room began to spin like the shadows around the rim of the mirror. The floor dropped away from under him, and he was whirled down into the darkness.

12

He was taking dinner to Mr. Hawkins. The dinner was all but hidden beneath the stack of mirrors he was carrying with it on the tray. He tramped up the walk to the old man's house. It had begun to grow dark, and there were lights on inside.

He set the tray down on the wicker table so he could ring the bell. Peeking through the curtains, he saw Mr. Hawkins sitting in his chair. His shoes were muddy; the carpet was stained where he'd crossed it.

He rapped on the window, but the old man didn't move. He rapped again, so hard he shivered the glass. Mr. Hawkins stirred and stretched. Turning to the window, he motioned for Simon to come in.

"No need to knock so hard, lad," he said as Simon stepped into the room with the loaded tray.

"I knocked and knocked and you didn't move," said Simon. "I thought you were dead."

"Dead? Hardly. More alive than I've felt in ages, actually. Just having a little nap, that's all. I've been working hard in the *garden with Eleanor, cutting and weeding and planting. The place has all gone to rack and ruin, she says." He examined the perfectly ordinary little mirrors Simon had brought from his house, as if they were precious artifacts.*

"But I thought Eleanor was dead."

"You seem to think everyone is dead, Simon. Are you sure you're feeling quite well? You look a little peaked."

A sound of clattering came from the kitchen.

"That'll be Eleanor washing up," said Mr. Hawkins. "Why don't you take these in to her?"

Simon gathered up the mirrors and carried them to the kitchen. Eleanor stood at the sink. She was wearing a wide-brimmed sunhat and gardening gloves. All the mirrors in the house had been taken down and were heaped on the floor and table and countertop. She was washing them one by one in the sudsy water and setting them on the dish rack to dry.

"Hello, Simon," she said, turning to him with a smile. "My, how you've grown. Just set those things down over there. These old mirrors have gotten so dingy you can barely see yourself in them.

"There now. Nothing a good cleaning won't cure." And up out of the water she pulled the Egyptian mirror, and held it dripping in the air.

He gasped in shock, and the mirrors slipped from his hands and fell crashing to the floor.

Simon woke with a start, the sound of shattering mirrors still loud in his ears. His heart raced, and his breath came short and sharp. Muted light seeped through the drawn curtains. A sheet lay draped over the dresser mirror. The dream seemed infinitely more real than this shadowed room he'd woken to. If he hurried to the window he would find the lights on still in the Hawkins house.

But sleep wrapped its leaden arms around him and urged him under. He had surfaced countless times like this since they'd brought him home from the memorial service and put him to bed—rising briefly to a sound, a light, a face hovering over his, a hand upon his forehead, a voice speaking his name, then sinking back into that dark embrace like a stone dropped in a bottomless pool. Christmas came and went. They put a tiny plastic tree in his room. The lights flickered like beacons on an un-approachable coast.

Never had he felt such fatigue. Fatigue so profound that simply to turn his body from one side to the other in the bed demanded more energy than he could possibly muster; so profound that breathing itself was an effort, keeping his eyelids from fluttering closed an impossibili-ty. He began to think he would never wake up again.

He fought against it now, forced himself to sit up and swing his legs over the side of the bed. The room did a slow spin around him. His head throbbed, and his throat was sore. When he reached up to feel his neck, he found the glands swollen and tender to the touch. Every muscle in his body ached.

The floor was ice against his feet when he went to stand. The cold surged through him like an electric cur-rent and set his teeth to chattering. His legs could barely support his weight. He took two unsteady steps, clinging to the bed for support. Step by tentative step he made his way to the window and drew back the curtain.

The shuddery old window was rimmed with ice. The world, shrunken down to shadow and dream, swelled with substance before his wondering eyes. He felt as if he'd returned from a long, dark voyage. Everything seemed new and strange. The fresh-fallen snow lay shimmering like diamonds over all, each tree branch delicately frosted as if by hand.

The snow was scored with tracks all up and down the street, but around the Hawkins house it lay unbroken still. Time and again in his dreams he had visited the old house. His wandering soul had worn a path to its door. But in this waking world it stood solitary and still. No smoke plumed from its chimney. No lights shone inside. The snow draped the roof like a pall.

Mom came into the room, amazed to find him up. She emptied the old wingback chair that sat against the wall and drew it over into the bay of the window.

"It's so good to see you up, Simon," she said. "We've been worried sick about you. It's been over two weeks now you've been in bed. Now you just sit here and soak up some of that lovely sun while I strip the sheets and change the bed."

She talked nonstop as she tidied the room and changed the sheets, while he sat shivering with cold, staring out the window. He found the talk too loud, the words too quick to cling to. He let it flow over him as if it were another language.

"I'll just take this old thing off here now, shall I?" she said and was about to slip the sheet off the dresser mirror.

"No, don't. Please," he pleaded.

The distress in his voice made her stop. "Okay. We'll just leave it for now, shall we?"

She chatted on, but there was a note of unease in her voice now. All was not as well as she'd imagined. When she was done, she helped him back into bed, drew the curtains closed as he'd asked, and closed the door quietly behind her as she left.

He lay exhausted in the shadowed room as the silence settled back over things, and his whirling thoughts came to rest.

His eye fell on the dresser mirror. It was quite safe now that it was covered. But one day, in the timeless time since illness struck, he'd woken in the dim room to find the mirror emptied of its reflections, and a faint, familiar form huddled in the shadows by the dresser, peering boldly back at him through his own eyes. He'd screamed out in terror and frightened it back into the mirror where it belonged.

When Mom came rushing into the room to see what was the matter, he'd been unable to settle until she covered the mirror with a sheet. There it had stayed, and there it would continue to stay until he felt well enough to take it down.

13

By January, with still no sign of improvement, the family doctor was summoned. He examined Simon, drew blood, ran tests, tried to unravel the riddle of his illness. He said his white blood cell count was high, his iron low; it was clear he was fighting something, though he couldn't say what.

He set up appointments with specialists. Over the next few weeks, Mom ferried Simon around in taxis from one to the next. They pricked him and poked him, palpated the tender nodes on his neck, noted the weakness in his muscles.

They took urine samples, drew countless vials of blood, ordered X-rays, ultrasounds, ECGs, MRIs. They eliminated the likely candidates—hepatitis and mononucleosis. Ruled out the direst possibilities—Lyme disease, leukemia, and multiple sclerosis.

But whatever lay at the root of his illness was a mystery to them. He showed no clinical evidence of infection or disease. Some were confused, others skeptical. One specialist wondered aloud about "a possible psychological cause" underlying his symptoms. Had there been some recent trauma or emotional shock? When Mom mentioned Mr. Hawkins' death, he nodded knowingly. A few weeks rest and Simon should be back up and running, as good as new, he assured them.

"Now, don't drive yourself too hard, young man," he told Simon.

Drive himself too hard? It had taken him ten minutes that morning to make the short trip from his room to the taxi waiting out front. He returned from the appointment utterly exhausted, crawled back into bed in the dim, silent room, and slept the sleep of the dead the rest of the day.

Convinced her son was now on the mend, Mom swept in cheerfully the next morning with a big breakfast on the silver tray. She threw back the curtains to let in the light, and opened the window a crack to air the room. But the light hurt his eyes, and the icy whisper of wind through the crack chilled him to the bone. As soon as she left he hauled himself out of bed and went to close them both.

Trying to be helpful, Dad carried an old portable TV up from the cellar and hooked it up in his room. He was pleased with how many channels he could bring in. But the frantic dance of images, the din of voices, and the manic onslaught of ads left Simon dizzy and dazed. Within minutes of Dad's leaving, he switched it off. A few days later, tired of looking at it lingering expectantly at the foot of the bed, reflecting him in its great glass eye, he draped it with his dressing gown and banished it to the corner of the room.

They brought him books—but to read was unthinkable. His eyes could not negotiate the page; could not complete the perilous crossing from left to right, the hazardous descent from summit to base. They inched uncertainly along the narrow ledge of words, tumbled repeatedly from one line to the next, tried desperately to scramble back, and lost all sense of meaning in the process. The books sat unread on the shelf by his bed and merged swiftly into the landscape of the room.

Days flowed into weeks, with little sign of recovery. School by now was a distant memory. His major accomplishment each morning was to make the arduous trek from his bed to the window, where he'd sit in the wingback chair for several hours a day.

It was the end of January—the dead of winter in Caledon. Frost etched the edge of the windows with fractured patterns. The frigid wind snaked its way in through the cracks. He wore a pair of woolen socks under his slippers, a toque tugged down over his ears, a heavy hoodie zipped up tight over his pajama top, dark sunglasses against the painful glare of light.

Time had slowed to a sluggish crawl. Watching the neighbors shovel their walks was gripping drama now. The appearance of the postman at the end of the street to walk his round was a notable event. He gazed in rapt attention as a scruffy tomcat with a torn ear crossed the street and sauntered down the side of Miss Logan's house in quest of the scraps she laid out for the neighborhood strays.

He watched kids striking off to school in the morning,

straggling back in the afternoon; saw Joe Pimentel carefully shepherding the school age kids from his mom's daycare back and forth. One little girl stopped to make snow angels on the Hawkins lawn. She saw Simon sitting at the window and waved.

January slipped into February. Despite what the doctor had said, he was no more ready to return to school than fly to the moon. The farthest he'd been in weeks was to the bathroom at the end of the hall.

Each day was a mystery. One day, he'd wake up feeling clear and invigorated, only to crash when he pushed himself the least bit beyond his narrow bounds. The next, he'd wake up dull and mired in brain fog, the bed sheets soaked with sweat, every muscle in his body aching.

The doctors didn't think his condition was contagious, but just to be on the safe side around a child with an undeveloped immune system, Babs was not allowed in his room. Not that he was anywhere near being able to keep up with her at the moment, anyway. It took all the strength he could muster just to hold the spinning world still.

But several times a day, she toddled up the stairs and along the hall to his door. She fiddled vainly with the handle, then flopped down on her belly on the floor and called to him through the crack under the door.

"Dimon, Dimon," she'd say, reaching her pudgy fingers under the door as far as they would go. As she peeked with one eye through the crack, he'd creep up out of sight and pounce upon her waggling fingers. Squealing with delight, she'd snatch them away. Then, very slowly, she'd start to ease them under again—plucking them back time and again in trepidation.

They each delighted in the narrow gap beneath the door dividing them. They'd lie on the floor talking to one another as if it were the most natural thing in the world. She'd slide pieces of paper to him through the crack and roll crayons after them. He drew pictures and fed them back to her. She drew "picters" and passed them to him. He taped them to his side of the door, until the door was decked with Babs' pictures top to bottom. They rustled when the breeze caught them, fluttered and fell silent when someone entered or left the room.

One afternoon, he was lying across his bed reading the same paragraph for the third time in one of the books he'd plucked from the shelf when he heard Babs chattering away as she came along the hall. She gave her ritual twist of the door handle, then dropped to her belly and called to him under the door.

"Dimon," she giggled with stifled glee.

"What's up, Babs?" he said. He crossed the room and lay belly-down on the floor by the door. As he squinted through the crack he was startled to see two sets of eyes peering back.

"Dimon," squealed Babs excitedly, "Abbey."

And sure enough, there was Abbey, lying on the floor, peeking through the crack.

"You know, I don't think I've ever done this before," she said. "How are you feeling, Simon?"

"Better," he said. And he really did feel better because of seeing her.

"Abbey, go like dis," said Babs, and she reached her fingers under the door and waggled them, till Simon tickled them and she squealed and snatched them back.

Abbey reached her fingers under the door and waggled them as instructed. She giggled when he tickled them, but didn't draw them back. They looked at one another one-eyed under the door.

"I brought you something," she said. "Don't get too excited. It's schoolwork. It seems Miss Court was talking to your mom. Now that you're starting to feel a little better, she thought it would be a good idea to send a bit of work home to you, so that you don't fall too far behind. Since I live nearby, she asked if I'd mind bringing it."

She slid a couple of his notebooks and some handouts under the door.

"It's pretty straightforward," she said. "If you have any trouble with anything, just give me a call." She passed him a piece of paper with her name and number on it.

"Thanks, Abbey. How are things at school?" It felt like asking how life was on the dark side of the moon.

"Oh, same old game—hammerheads versus teachers. The hammerheads are winning. You couldn't *give* me enough money to be a teacher."

She reached her fingers under the door and brushed his hand. "It's good to see you, Simon. I should probably be going. Max will be wondering what happened to his favorite sister. I told him I'd take him tobogganing in the park when I got home."

"Max," said Babs.

"Yeah. Would you like to see Max again, Babs? I could maybe set you up."

They got up and headed hand in hand along the hall, Babs babbling nonstop all the while. Simon lay watching their feet through the crack, until they turned and disappeared down the stairs.

14

He was sitting by the window in the wingback chair. Abbey had pulled the desk chair up beside him. Her book bag stood propped against it. Her math book lay open on her lap.

"Okay, Simon, I need you to concentrate. I'll read it again: 'It's a stormy winter day. The school has decided to close early. The parents of all the children who go to the school need to be notified. The school has set up a system to do this. One parent calls three other parents. Then each of those calls three more. The pattern is repeated until all the parents have been informed of the early closing. How many parents will be called during the fourth set of calls?'"

Simon looked down at the worksheet. The diagram on it showed a pyramid of phones. The large phone at the top branched into three smaller ones beneath it. Those three branched into nine, smaller still. Those nine branched into a long row of tiny phones. He started to count them with his finger. Abbey reached out and lightly rapped his knuckle with her pencil.

"It's not about counting the tiny phones, Simon. It's about trying to find the pattern."

The problem was he couldn't find the pattern. Couldn't find the pattern to the pyramid of phones any more than he could find the pattern that had once held thoughts together in his head. It was all a jumble, like the inside of his closet—full of things pitched in at random. You opened the door and were never quite sure what might spill out.

Abbey had started dropping by for a while each day on her way home from school. She brought the homework Miss Court had prepared for him, along with the corrected work from the day before. He looked forward to her visits all afternoon. As kids began to drift by on their way back from school, he'd station himself at the window and wait for her to round the corner at the top of the street.

The first couple of times she ventured into his room, she wore a surgical mask her mom had given her so that she 'wouldn't catch whatever it was he had.' But *he* could barely make out her muffled words, and *she* could barely breathe. She finally ripped it off and tossed it in the waste-basket. She said she'd sooner die from whatever he had than from asphyxiation.

Her visits marked a turning point in his recovery. He was able to sit up a little longer each day in his chair; able to read a page or two without tumbling off the lines. For the first time in well over a month, he got out of his pajamas and got dressed.

Mom took it as a sign. Babs was allowed to come into his room now. They'd do puzzles together. Babs was a wiz with her puzzles. She *had* to show *him* where the pieces went. But after half an hour of doing puzzles with Babs, his head would start to spin. He'd have to shoo her from the room and lie down quietly in the dark until it stopped.

While he'd been sick, his room had quietly come undone. After the incident with the mirror, Mom didn't even bother trying to tidy it anymore. She just made a little whimper whenever she came into the room.

He tried straightening it up a little now himself, but the connections between things had been cut and reconfigured in strange ways in his sick mind. He found himself tucking the silver tray away in his sock drawer, hanging books up on hangers in the closet. He put some things away so well, he couldn't find them for weeks afterwards. In the end, he gave up and let chaos reign. The piles mounted unmolested around the fringes of the room.

He slipped the sheet from his dresser mirror and studied the gaunt stranger in the glass as he brushed his tousled hair. Sickness had stamped itself on his face. His eyelids drooped a little now and his mouth hung slightly open, giving him a kind of bewildered look.

"So one parent calls three others," said Abbey. "Those three each call three more, and the same pattern is repeated until all the parents are called. So—how many are called on the very first call?"

He peered down at the pyramid of telephones on the handout sheet and tried to focus. "Three?"

"*Good*," she said. She could tell it was a guess, but tried to be supportive. "And how many on the second?"

He ran his eyes over the second row of phones, counting under his breath.

"Those first three each call *three* more," she prompted.

"Nine?"

"*Yes*," she said, so loud he jumped. "And *that's* called three to the power of two. This is a problem that's supposed to teach us about powers, you see. Now how many are called on the third call?"

He looked down at the long row of tiny telephones running across the handout sheet. He was tempted to try and count them again, but she already had her pencil poised to rap his finger if he tried. As he stared down at the tiny phones they broke loose from their moorings and began to drift around the page. He looked out the window to steady himself.

Across the street the Hawkins house stood empty and still. Fliers were wedged in the porch rail. Mail bristled from the box. One of the gnarled limbs of the wisteria had broken loose in the big storm and hung in a slack festoon between the porch pillars, laden with snow. The wind chime stood mute, as if in mourning.

It saddened him to see the place coming slowly undone. He wanted to run across and tidy it up, return it to the way it had been before death passed by.

Inside, the house was just as it had always been. Part of him walked there still, fetching and carrying like an unquiet ghost. The cot still rested by the dining room table, the two chairs still sat side by side in the front room. The TV stood on its wheeled stand against the wall. The mirrors that filled the walls in the silent old house were still in their places. All save for one. He saw it in his mind's eye now, lying on the dining room table as the old man told his incredible tale.

Where is it now? he wondered again.

The math book lay facedown on Abbey's empty chair. She was standing with her back to him at the dresser, her face reflected in the mirror.

"You do that a lot, Simon, you know," she said. "Phase out. Wander off. Whatever you want to call it. One minute, you're here with me in the room. And then suddenly— you're not. I mean, you're still sitting there. Your eyes are open and everything, but you're gone. Where do you go? Where were you just now?"

He couldn't lie. "Over there," he said, nodding his head in the direction of the Hawkins house. "In the old house across the street. I'm there a lot."

She studied him in the mirror. "Is that the house where the old man lived?"

He nodded. "You see that photo there, in the corner of the mirror?"

"This one?" She pointed to the picture of the two boys on the porch steps.

"Yeah. That boy on the left is Mr. Hawkins."

"Who's the other boy?"

"My granddad."

"Wow—you *look* like him," she said, plucking the photo from the frame.

"'The spitting image,' Mr. Hawkins said."

She tucked the photo back in the frame and returned to her chair. She sat there quietly looking out the window, the math book open on her lap.

"How did he die?" she asked.

"Heart attack, they said."

He told her how Mr. Hawkins began to believe there were prowlers on his property. He talked about him phoning the house at night, his dad going over with the flashlight to look for them. But he didn't tell her about the letter.

He told her about the terrible day after the storm, how he'd been unable to get in touch with Mr. Hawkins to make sure he was all right, how he'd finally gone over with Babs and the lemon pudding cake and seen him through the window, sitting in his chair, still as stone. But he didn't tell her the most important thing—the thing that lay at the heart of it all.

It had taken Mr. Hawkins a long time to tell him about the Egyptian mirror. If the old man hadn't noticed he was able to see things in it, he might never have said anything at all. Simon understood now why it had been hard for him to talk about it. He understood his fear of seeming crazy.

When he was finally done talking, it was time for Abbey to go. She left the math problem with him. He figured out how many parents were called on the third call by counting the row above the tiny phones. But after that he was on his own. As he settled into bed that night, he still had no idea how many parents were phoned on the fourth call.

15

At the heart of the stillness surrounding the Hawkins house lay the missing will. It was clear there had been a will. At the memorial service, Joan Cameron told Mom that when she visited Mr. Hawkins a little more than a month before he died, he asked her to bring down the box of papers with the will in it from the desk in the study. He made some changes to it, and she witnessed his signature.

Later that day, Simon himself had put the box back in the desk. But when it was found there after the old man's death, the will wasn't in it. The court-appointed estate trustee went through the house with a fine-tooth comb hunting for it, but failed to turn it up.

In the absence of any known next of kin, the trustee posted a notice in the classified section of several regional and national newspapers over the next two months, asking that anyone related to the deceased, or with any knowledge of an extant will, contact the trustee at once. Weeks went by, and no one came forward.

Then, at the end of February, a rumor started up on the street that a relative had been found. For a long time it was simply a rumor.

Meanwhile, winter wrapped the old house in its cold white arms and rocked it to sleep. Simon began to think it would never wake up again. It would sit there empty and still as the seasons rolled over it, and become the abode of ghosts.

Babs' scream jolted Simon from his sleep. He hurried down the hall to her room. The nightlight cast its pale beam on the wall by her bed. She was standing in her crib, one leg flung up onto the rail. He could hear the fear in her wailing.

Mom's sleepy voice straggled up the stairs. "Is she all right, Simon?"

"Another bad dream," he said. "I'll settle her."

He switched on the lamp and saw her eyes, wide with panic. She looked right through him as he approached her. He eased her leg down off the rail.

"It's all right, Babs," he said. "It was just a bad dream."

But no words he said could reach her. She was somewhere else. Between them lay the unbridgeable chasm of dream. He could not cross to her, or she to him. Her body stood here in the crib, but her soul had wandered, and was caught in the grip of a nightmare.

He picked her up and patted her back as he walked her up and down the room. Sometimes, when she got like this, she wouldn't even let you hold her. She'd arch her back, scream and flail, and no amount of comforting would calm her. If you tried to reason with her, her only response was a wild-eyed look. If you lost patience, her panic spiraled even further out of control.

She was cutting her two-year molars. Her gums were sore, and her sleep was shallow and unsettled. She would surface suddenly while in the midst of a dream and only seem to be awake.

Simon could understand that. At the worst of his sickness he'd spent weeks straddling the border between sleeping and waking, never quite sure which country he was in. Half-awake while sleeping, half-asleep while awake, the boundary between the two hopelessly blurred.

He paced up and down the shadowy room. Gradually, her breathing grew calmer. She laid her head on his shoulder and tucked her thumb in her mouth. He lowered her into the crib, covered her, switched off the lamp, and tip-toed toward the door.

Suddenly, she sat bolt upright in the bed, muttering something about the "woo-woo," the "bad woo-woo."

"It's all right, Babs," he said. "The bad doggie's all gone."

She looked over at him—for the first time truly *looked* at him. "Aw gone," she repeated and lay back down. He stood by the door till her breathing deepened and she dropped off.

An hour later, he still hadn't managed to fall back to sleep. Babs' fright had loosed the floodgates of memory and brought the incident with the dog back to his mind. Every time he closed his eyes he found himself back in the Hawkins' yard, poking at the bushes with the handle of the hoe, then suddenly feeling his blood run cold as that low growl sounded from the shadows.

The sound merged now in his mind with the rumble of a car stereo outside. He waited for it to roll on by. When it didn't, he slipped out of bed and went to the window to see what was up. A sleek black car had pulled up to the curb across the road. It sat there with its headlights dimmed and music pulsing in the darkened cab.

Suddenly, the sound died and the lights went dark. For a long minute there was nothing but silence. Then the door opened on the driver's side and a lean figure stepped out, took a quick look around, and then went round to the passenger side and opened the door.

A woman emerged. She was tall and thin and had on a fur coat and matching hat. Though it was the middle of the night, she was wearing dark glasses. She took the lead as they proceeded slowly along the street and turned up the walk to the Hawkins house. They moved with a light, liquid gait. Though she wore heels, there was no sound.

The wind chime—silent till then—started up its broken song as they stepped up onto the porch. She looked up at it and said something to her companion. He reached up and with a quick yank plucked it down, walked over to the rail of the porch, and dropped it into the garden below.

She turned and took a long look up and down the street, running her eyes slowly over the houses. Though it was dark in his room, Simon slunk back from the window and didn't stir until he heard the Hawkins front door opening. He peeked out and saw them disappear into the house and close the door behind them.

A light winked on inside. He pictured them standing in the hall, felt the soft tread of their footsteps on the worn runner, imagined them turning into the front room, then saw another light as the lamp was flicked on. He felt their footsteps as they moved about the room, imagined their gaze falling on the sections of manuscript, the drift of books he had carried down the stairs.

He felt them slide silently up the stairs to the second floor. A light came on in the front bedroom. Their shadows flitted ghostlike on the curtained window. A few minutes later, the light came on in the study at the rear of the house, spilling its glow down onto the snow in the yard below.

When they emerged half an hour later, the man was carrying a cardboard box. She locked the door behind them and went back to the car. He dumped the box in the back and got in behind the wheel. The engine started up, and with it the low throb of the stereo. It hung in the air like a heartbeat as the car drifted off slowly down the street.

16

There were good days. There were bad days. They were completely unpredictable. But from the moment he opened his eyes in the morning, he knew which it would be. When he woke the following morning, there was a sharp, coppery taste in his mouth and a dull throbbing in his head that stirred the memory of the car in the night. When he sat up, the room whirled. It was definitely a bad day.

He got dressed and made his way slowly down the stairs, gripping the handrail. He felt as fragile as the old mirrors gathering dust in the Hawkins house.

Mom was rushing around getting ready for work. She was going to drop Babs off at Mrs. Pimentel's on the way, and was trying to coax her to put on her shoes. Babs was a creature of routine, and this definitely wasn't part of her routine. She was supposed to be sitting watching her cartoons with a bowl of dry cereal and some "appa dew" in her sippy cup, as she usually did at this time in the morning.

"Don't you want to go see all the kids at Mrs. Pimentel's?" said Mom as she tried to wiggle the shoe on over Babs' scrunched-up foot. "Luca will be there, and Lizzie. It'll be lots of fun."

Babs wasn't buying it. Going over to Mrs. "Pim-tel's" from time to time was all right, she supposed, but no one had consulted her about missing her morning shows and spending the whole day there. But now that Mom was working full days at the Busy Bee to cover for a cashier on maternity leave, there wasn't much choice.

Mom finally managed to wiggle the shoe onto Babs' foot. She gave her face a wipe with a wet cloth and scooped her up. "You're *sure* you'll be all right here alone, Simon?"

"Don't worry. I'll be fine."

"Okay," she said with a sigh. "Remember, Dad will be here around noon to take you to the appointment." She gave him a peck on the cheek and was out the door with Babs on her hip.

He shuffled into the living room and lay down on the couch. Their things stood awkwardly around the edges of the redecorated room like boys at a school dance: the small wooden bookcase bristling with paperback romances and drugstore thrillers, the tattered couch, the coffee table ringed with stains where Dad set down his drink when he watched TV.

The remnant of Granddad's things helped raise the tone: the china cupboard with its glass doors and fancy dishes, the full-length mirror in its frame, the old upright piano that stood against the wall opposite the couch. As he stared dully across at it now, his brain mired in fog, he saw the shade of a younger Simon sitting there on the bench while Granddad guided his fingers over the ivory keys. Ghostly music filled the room.

Shortly before noon, Dad arrived to take him to the appointment. One of the regular customers at the butcher shop was a doctor at a nearby clinic. The subject of Simon's mysterious illness had come up in conversation, and the doctor suggested that Dad bring him by to see him.

It was well into March now, and the recovery that the doctors had predicted for Simon had not occurred. The school authorities were becoming concerned over his extended absence, and Simon could see questions starting to creep into his parents' eyes. Was he *really* sick, or was it something else?

The waiting room at the clinic was too crowded, the fluorescent lights too bright, the TV hanging in the corner too loud. He retreated to the quiet of the hall until Dad came to tell him the doctor was ready to see him.

The doctor was friendly and informal, and had something of the rugged good looks of a young Mr. Hawkins about him. Several mountain pictures hung on the walls of his office. Dad had said he was a professional climber and had been a member of several expeditions on some of the world's highest mountains.

He had a thick file on his desk with the results of all the tests Simon had already had. As he leafed through it he glanced up at Simon.

"Looks like they've been 'round the block with you," he said.

After he finished going through the file, he gave Simon a thorough examination—shone a light in his eyes, looked in his mouth, felt the tender nodes in his neck, took his blood pressure, asked countless questions about his sleep and his ongoing struggles with fogginess and fatigue. Finally, he sat down on the edge of the desk, folded his arms over his chest, and gave him a long look.

"You sure you haven't been climbing any mountains lately?" he said.

Simon couldn't help but smile as he shook his head.

"Because if I didn't know better," he went on, "I'd say you were suffering from hypoxia—what people call altitude sickness. It's marked by a feeling of profound exhaustion, coupled with a sense of confusion and disorientation. It's caused by a lack of oxygen, and is usually cured by administering the gas from a tank, and descending to a lower altitude as quickly as possible. It looks to me like you're climbing some nasty internal mountain, Simon.

"I don't know what's causing your sickness, but I suspect it's a virus of some sort. Viruses are invisible invaders. They can hide, mutate, combine, and elude detection. They can lie dormant in the body, waiting to be set off by sudden stress or some environmental trigger or other. This looks a lot like mononucleosis to me. The tests say it's not—but I suspect it's likely related. Now, mono can take a long time to get over, and I think this might, too.

"I'm going to run a couple more tests," he said to Dad. "But I'm pretty sure they're going to come back negative like the others. It looks unlikely to me at this stage that Simon will get back to school before the fall. I'll write a letter with my diagnosis for you to pass along to the principal of the school. I'm sure they'll be open to continuing the arrangement you've made to have work sent home for him.

"I want you to be sure you eat well, and get your rest, Simon. Do what you can, but don't push it. The last thing you want is a relapse."

17

"Altitude sickness? That's interesting," said Abbey when Simon told her later that day. She said she'd be happy to keep bringing work home for him till he managed to get down the mountain.

They were sitting by the window in his room. She was trying to explain the science homework to him. He found it hard to concentrate on what she was saying. As he looked across at the Hawkins house, his mind kept replaying the events of the night before.

"Okay, Simon," she said, knuckling her glasses back up to the bridge of her nose, "you're supposed to look at this forest scene and the various plants and animals in it. Then you have to answer these questions here."

"Someone was at the Hawkins house last night," he said.

She looked up from the text. "Pardon?"

"Two people came by late last night in a car—a man and a woman. They went into the house, went all through it. They were there for quite a while."

"Must be those relatives they found," she said and

turned back to the homework. "Okay, so the first thing to do is look at the picture and divide the things you see into producers and consumers. So, for instance, the pine tree there is a producer. That wolf over there is a consumer. It's dead simple."

"They were strange," he said.

She closed the book on her finger to keep her place. "Strange how?"

"I don't know, just strange. It was *midnight*—and she was wearing shades. And there was something weird about the way they walked."

"Weird how?"

"They didn't make any noise. It was like they were floating."

"*Floating*?" She gave him a long look over the top of her glasses.

"They were in there for nearly an hour; just moving from one room to the next—like they were looking for something."

"Looking for what?"

"I don't know. Something." *Something like the Egyptian mirror*, he wanted to say. But that was the part of the story he hadn't told her.

"Don't you think you may be imagining things? They were probably just seeing what the place looked like."

"Maybe," he said doubtfully.

He tried to pay attention as she explained how a sudden decline in the wolf population due to overhunting could affect the balance of the entire forest ecosystem. But all he kept seeing when he looked down at the page was the woman in shades standing on the porch, scanning the houses along the street.

The visits went on. Several times a week, late at night, he'd hear the rumble of the car stereo and slip to his window to watch as the dark car drew up in front of the house. Often, they had a load of empty boxes with them. They stayed about an hour, usually. Periodically, the man came out carrying a box. Sometimes he'd put it in the car, sometimes add it to the mounting pile on the porch.

Simon would have given a lot to know exactly what they were up to as they moved methodically through the house; exactly what was in those boxes accumulating on the porch. They sat there stacked against the wall in all weather. When a freak snowstorm blew in at the end of March, they were blanketed in windblown snow for several days. He was tempted to go over and brush them off so that whatever was in them wouldn't be ruined. Abbey said that would *not* be a good idea.

Speculation swirled on the street as to who the new people might be. Someone had heard from someone else that it was Eleanor Hawkins' niece, but for now it was all just speculation.

One night at the beginning of April, on the eve of garbage day, the car came by a little earlier than usual. This time the guy was alone. He didn't bother going into the house. He just went up onto the porch and hauled all the boxes that were stacked there down to the curb for the morning collection. Then he got back in the car and drove off.

For a long while Simon looked at the boxes sitting by the curb. Finally, he went and plucked the piece of paper with Abbey's number on it from the mirror frame and picked up the phone.

"Hey, Abbey," he said when she answered. "I had a question about the science homework."

"Nice try, Simon. What is it?"

"I need to ask you a favor."

"Do you have any idea what time it is, Simon?"

"Sorry, but this is important, Abbey. I need your help with something."

"What is it?"

"Well—you know those boxes that have been piling up on the Hawkins porch?"

"You can't *take* them, Simon. We've been over this before."

"No, listen. The guy came by tonight. He put them all down at the curb for the garbage collection tomorrow morning. They're sitting there now."

There was a pause—a *long* pause. "You're completely insane. You know that, don't you, Simon?"

"Yeah, I know. Hey, could you maybe bring Max's wagon with you?"

She swore into the phone and hung up. He wasn't sure she'd come. But twenty minutes later, he heard the *bumpity-bump* of the wagon coming down the street.

He quickly pulled on his things and opened the window wide enough to climb out. Once, in the summer, when he was playing ball with the guys, Joe had hammered a ball that came down on the porch roof and lodged in the gutter.

Simon had to scale the old trellis anchored to the porch post to fetch it.

He crept across the roof now, took hold of the top of the trellis, gave it a shake to make sure it was secure, then scrambled down in the dark, praying the rickety thing wouldn't break.

Abbey came padding along the street in her slippers, pulling the little wagon behind her. She had her jacket on over her pajamas.

"Don't say a word, Simon—not a *word*. You might find this hard to believe, but some people actually *sleep* at night." She looked over at the boxes piled at the curb. "Let's get this done," she said.

The boxes were heavy. There was no way he could have moved them alone. They loaded four onto the little wagon, then hauled them across the street and down the dimly-lit lane to the garage. He pulled and she pushed, the wagon creaking under the weight of the boxes, the wheels juddering over the loose stones in the lane. He thought about how the guy had plucked them up off the porch and carried them down to the curb two at a time as if they weighed nothing.

With the first load safely stowed away inside the garage, they went back for the second. They were lifting the last of the boxes into the wagon when he heard a low distant rumble. He stiffened like he'd been shot. The box slipped from his hands and dropped with a thud into the wagon.

"Take it easy, will you, Simon? If someone sees us and calls the cops, we're going to have a whole lot of explaining to do."

"Shhh," he said. "Do you hear that?" His eyes panned nervously up and down the street.

"Hear what?"

"That low pulsing sound." Off in the distance he saw the twin beams of a car's headlights piercing the darkness like a pair of luminous eyes.

"Yeah, it's called a car stereo. Honestly, Simon, you're starting to give me the creeps. Let's just get this stuff into the garage, okay? I've got to get back home before my folks miss me."

He took one last look down the street. The lights winked out. The music died.

"There," she said. "Satisfied?"

He glanced back at the house. "Hang on a sec." He scooted up the walk and fished around blindly in the garden in front of the porch. He pulled out the wind chime, and came tinkling down the walk with it.

Abbey rolled her eyes. This time she pulled the wagon, while he pushed from behind. The wheels jumped and jived along the lane. Somewhere down the shadowy corridors of his mind he could still hear the low, sinister pulse of the stereo.

Satisfied? No—not by a long shot.

18

The lock hung loose in the hasp as he'd left it. Inside, the rescued boxes sat in two piles on the packed-dirt floor. The wind chime lay across one. Scrambling on top of an old dresser, he hung it from the rafters on a rusty hook, then scattered the boxes among Granddad's things till they blended in.

Over the next few weeks, while he was home alone during the day, he hauled them, one by one, up to his room. As he finished with each, he marked the box, returned it to the garage.

The work was slow and taxing. His store of energy was measured out in meager doses. The added exertion drained him, leaving his body limp and his mind muddled. His muzzy brain was like a busy bus depot; thoughts arrived at random, stopped over briefly, departed abruptly. He'd think of something he wanted to tell Abbey, and then forget it entirely as it boarded the next bus out of his brain.

He began writing notes to remind himself. The words came out fractured, the letters back to front. Soon the room was strewn with scraps of scribbled paper. He'd come upon them and stand over them, trying to puzzle them out. He reminded himself more and more of Mr. Hawkins with his cryptic notes, his conviction that things were not as they seemed, his belief that something sinister was afoot—and it all somehow had something to do with the Egyptian mirror.

Each box was a revelation. One especially heavy one proved to be packed with the Hawkins photo albums that had sat on the low shelf in the living room. Mr. Hawkins had said Eleanor was a demon for photo albums. The albums were painstakingly arranged, the photos annotated in her small precise script, their life together meticulously chronicled. He kept thinking of how close they'd come to being lost forever.

One afternoon, Abbey arrived to find the bed covered in stacks of paper arranged in orderly rows, and Simon flitting from one to another, a sheaf of loose pages in his hand.

"You won't believe what I found in the box I brought in today," he said as he fanned through a pile and slid a few of the stray pages home.

She put down her bag and wandered over to take a closer look. "What is it?" she asked.

"Mr. Hawkins' *book*," he said excitedly. "He had it laid out in piles like this in his study upstairs. I used to bring down sections for him to work on. I think it's all here. Do you know how long he'd been working on this book? Years and years, and they were just going to toss it all in the trash."

Abbey picked up a section and fanned through it, pausing to read a paragraph or two. "Looks interesting. What
are you going to do with it?"

"Read it, to start with. Then, I'm not sure. Maybe there's
some way to get it published." He felt a little lightheaded
suddenly, and went to sit down.

"You're working too hard on this, Simon," said Abbey.
"Remember what the doctor said. You need to take it
easy." She pulled her chair up next to his and began rooting through her bag for the homework sheets.

Simon looked across at the old house. The spring sun
had melted most of the snow from the lawn. The grass lay
limp and pale. As he looked at the stretch of the yard running along the side of the house he saw the hoe still lying
where he'd dropped it the day he went looking for the dog.
The memory surged back in all its terror. He had to tell
her—tell her now.

"They're not who they say they are."

Abbey looked up, surprised. "Who?"

"The new people. Think about it, Abbey. If you'd just
inherited a house from your uncle, would the first thing
you'd do be to throw out the manuscript of a book he'd
been working on for years?"

"Maybe they didn't know what else to do with it."

"Or maybe they didn't care. And what about those photo albums? If she *were* Eleanor Hawkins' niece, there'd be
photos of her family in there. Why would she just chuck
them all out like that?"

"Who are they then?"

"There's something I didn't tell you," he said.

"Oh?"

"There was this mirror in the Hawkins house—"

"You told me about the mirrors, Simon. Remember?"

"Not this one," he said. "This one was different from the rest. It hung in the living room, opposite the chair Mr. Hawkins' wife used to sit in. I noticed it the first time I brought dinner to him. It was a bronze mirror, but unlike the others, it shone. Most of the time it was just an ordinary mirror. But sometimes, I—I *saw* things in it. Visions, I guess you'd call them. Look, all this must sound completely crazy."

"Go on," she said.

"They never lasted long. Just a glimpse, really, and then they'd be gone. It was like I was looking down in a dark pool. Once, I saw a face rising up through the water. Another time, I saw someone running by moonlight through the desert, with the mirror under his arm. I saw an eye open in the mirror, and then a figure flowed out of it and fell onto the sand."

"That's scary, Simon," she said.

"Mr. Hawkins sensed I could see things in the mirror. The last time I saw him, he told me his wife Eleanor had been able to see things in it, too. Then he told me how they'd come by it."

Simon told Abbey the whole story, from the dealer Winstanley approaching Eleanor at the conference about an old Egyptian mirror rumored to possess magical powers, to them going to his shop to see it, and ultimately buying it and bringing it back home with them.

He told her about the letter from London that Mr. Hawkins had received shortly before he died, in which

Winstanley confessed there were things he hadn't told them about the mirror when they bought it. He told her about the mysterious woman at the auction, the dreams that troubled Winstanley's sleep once the mirror was in his possession, the dreadful presence he felt pursuing him, and the plan he hatched to pawn the mirror off on them.

"Wait," he said. He went to his dresser and fished around at the back of one of the drawers. He came out holding an envelope and handed it to her.

"What's this?" She opened it, looked down at the blotchy, rippled pages.

"It's the letter."

"What happened to it?"

"It got a little wet."

"Yeah."

"You can still read it—most of it, anyway. On that last night, Mr. Hawkins told me he believed the mirror possessed some sort of power, and was afraid of it falling into the wrong hands. Then he was dead, and the mirror had vanished. At the memorial service, his friend Joan Cameron told me he'd talked about hiding it. I think it's still there somewhere. I think that's what those new people are looking for. I can't help feeling it's up to me to find it first, if I can, and keep it safe."

All that evening he wondered if he'd done the right thing in telling her about the mirror. She thought he was weird enough already. He was afraid she wouldn't want anything more to do with him now.

Around nine-thirty the phone rang. It was Abbey.

"I've read that letter about a dozen times, Simon, and

each time it's creepier. I keep thinking about that woman at the auction. I knew I wouldn't sleep a wink if I didn't call you. I've been thinking a lot about what you said. I believe you did see something in that mirror, just like Mr. Hawkins' wife did. I think it does possess some sort of power, and maybe these people are after it because of that. We really don't know for sure.

"I'll do whatever I can to help you, Simon. I figure two of us are better than one. But you need to trust me. No more secrets, okay?"

With spring in the air, birdsong woke him most days at dawn. Birds of all kinds flocked in the overgrown cedars separating the Hawkins yard from the cat lady's next door. Whenever one of Mrs. Logan's strays appeared on the scene, the bushes erupted in a flurry of wings.

Spears of green sprang up in the gardens along the street as daffodils and tulips reappeared. Mr. Glover stripped the burlap shroud off his bushes and raked the matted leaves from his lawn. Dad fetched the garden shears from the shed and trimmed the high hedge that ran across the front of their property. Down at the end of the street the gang started playing baseball again.

Simon sat in the wingback chair observing all. He drew deep drafts of the rich, earthy air. The numbing fog that filled his brain began to lift, and there were blessed days when he could think clearly again. He felt like those long-buried plants pushing up into the light, spreading their leaves in the sun.

Once he'd managed to reassemble the "Soul Catchers" manuscript, he began to work his way through it. It was tough going. Mr. Hawkins hadn't had sick Simon in mind when he wrote it. But as he sat by the window with a chapter on his lap, he could almost hear the old man's voice as he read:

> The ancients believed that all people were born double. Although the double possessed substance, it was made of so delicate a stuff that it was normally hidden from sight. The ancient Egyptians called this double the ka.
>
> In the ancient temple at Luxor, a series of relief sculptures show the birth of the pharaoh Amenophis. While two goddesses serving as midwives attend the king's mother, two others are shown carrying two newborn children away. The inscriptions above them indicate that the first of these is the actual child, the second the double.
>
> The double was immortal. After the body's death, it lived on. As the source of one's life and individuality, it was essential that the ka remain by the mummy until such time as it awoke and, gazing on its double, was magically revivified and able to pass into the afterworld. Scholars believe that a mirror may have served as a home for the ka in the tomb. It may even have served as a portal to the afterworld.
>
> This would explain why mirrors played such an important role in Egyptian burial customs. The

presence of mirrors in burials was not restricted to
the nobility. Common people as well were regularly
buried with mirrors, even if only of painted wood.
The mirror was placed in the hands or on the breast
of the mummy, or so positioned in the tomb that it
would be the first thing the person would look upon
when they awoke.

The mirror was a visible sign of the sun god Ra's
presence and his magical power of bringing life
from death. But it may have served a more prac-
tical purpose as well. By providing a home for the
double in the tomb, the mirror prevented it from
wandering off into the world and causing mischief
among the living.

Simon set the manuscript down. He went to the dresser
mirror and looked at his double, who looked questioningly
back. He touched his eyes, then his nose and his mouth,
and watched closely as the double did the same.

19

With the end of the school year in sight, Abbey began prepping Simon for the final exams. His reading had improved, but math was still a major challenge. Like the squirrels with their nuts, he tucked facts and formulas away and was unable to find them afterwards. The harder he searched, the more muddled they became. Scatter a twenty-piece puzzle on the floor, and he stood a pretty good chance of beating Babs at putting it back together. Ask him to find the area of an isosceles triangle, and he was hopelessly lost.

After the thrill of finding the Soul Catchers manuscript, he found the last few boxes he had hauled up to his room a letdown. One was full of old archaeological journals— some dating back nearly fifty years, their pages as brittle as dried leaves. He scanned the contents page of each issue and fanned through it to see if anything important might have been tucked between the pages. Dipping in briefly here and there, he found it dry as dust. More than once he ended up nodding off in his chair with the magazine splayed open on his lap.

Waking after one such sleep, he happened to glance over at the Hawkins house, and saw something odd—a faint glint in the stretch of garden that ran along the side the old house. A few days later he noticed it again. It would suddenly be there, then just as suddenly be gone. He couldn't figure out what it could be.

Then one day he happened upon an article by Randall Hawkins—it was the dashing photo of the young professor that first caught his attention—in an old issue of *The Journal of Biblical Archaeology*. It concerned the recent discovery of a cache of silver coins and precious jewels that had been buried in clay jars outside the walls of the ancient Biblical city of Gibeon.

Because of the frequent wars that swept over Palestine, he wrote, *people resorted to burying their valuables to safeguard them. In the ancient Middle East, burial was believed to be the best protection against thieves, and buried treasure is a recurring theme in the folklore of the region.*

A sudden stillness fell over the room—as if it were encased in glass. He heard the thunderous ticking of the clock on top of the dresser, the fretful buzzing of a fly as it circled the room, seeking a way out. The words looped around in his mind, like the trapped fly.

He glanced out the window at the old house. Mr. Hawkins was convinced there were those who had their sights set on the mirror and would stop at nothing to obtain it. Simon remembered what the old man had said to him about not allowing that to happen, what he'd told Cameron about hiding it. He pictured the faint trail leading across the carpet to where the figure sat still as stone, the dried mud on the side of his shoe. Suddenly, all the pieces fell into place.

The fly was *bump-bumping* against the window. He reached over and opened it—and out it flew.

He could hardly wait to tell Abbey the news. But the afternoon dragged endlessly by. Unable to bear it any longer, he threw on some clean clothes and headed off to meet her.

He took the route they used to take when he walked home from school with her, along the quiet, winding streets on the far side of the park. Before his sickness, he could have walked it in his sleep. But now, in no time at all, he became hopelessly lost. He felt as if he'd been flung down in some alien landscape—enticingly familiar, yet impossibly altered. He wandered aimlessly with no idea of where to turn next, growing increasingly frantic as fatigue overtook him.

At last, he came upon a place he recognized: a park they passed on the way. He collapsed on a bench like a castaway washed up on shore. He closed his eyes and dozed off where he sat. Suddenly, he was jarred into consciousness at the sound of his name.

"Simon? I *thought* it was you. What on earth are you doing here?"

It was Abbey. Now that he'd finally found her he tried to spill his news out all at once. The words tumbled out on top of one another.

"I was coming to meet you. I got a bit lost. I need to tell you something. I—I think I figured it out."

"Slow down, Simon. Figured what out?"

"Where he *hid* it."

The bench was close to the street. Kids on their way home from school were passing by. A couple looked their way.

"Tell you what, Simon," said Abbey. "Let's sit down over there in the shade, and you can tell me all about it, okay?"

She steered him farther into the park, away from the traffic and the passers-by. They sat on a bench under a tree. The park opened out around them on all sides in a sea of green.

"Don't move," she said. "I'll be right back."

She sprinted out to the street and crossed to a store on the corner. A few minutes later she returned with two cans of pop.

She popped the tab on one and handed it to him. "Drink," she said.

He took two long swallows, and realized for the first time how thirsty he'd been. Suddenly aware of the sweat rolling down his face, he reached up and wiped it off on his sleeve. The sweet, cool drink did its work, and in a couple of minutes he'd recovered.

"I guess I was a little excited," he said.

"I *guess*." He followed her gaze as she glanced down at his feet. He was wearing a sneaker on one foot and a slipper on the other.

"You're sort of half inside, half out," she said. "Now start again—from the beginning, Simon. You think you figured out where he hid it. Where *who* hid *what*?"

"Where Mr. Hawkins hid the mirror," he said. His eyes panned the park. A woman was playing fetch with a dog and a rubber ball. He watched as the dog made an incredible leap to snap the ball out of the air on a bounce. These days, anyone with a dog drew his attention. He studied them for a minute, then turned back to Abbey.

"*Focus*, Simon. The mirror, remember?"

"They can search the house all they want," he said. "They won't find it."

"Why?"

"Because it's not in the house."

"Where is it then?"

"I was going through those old journals I showed you the other day and I came across an article written by Mr. Hawkins." He told her what he'd read in the article, and paused to let it sink in. She gave him a blank look.

"Don't you see?" he said. "Mr. Hawkins was an archaeologist. He spent his life digging up things, things that in many cases had been buried to keep them safe. So when he felt the mirror was in danger—"

"He *buried* it."

"Exactly."

"Where?"

"In his yard. I think he'd probably already planned it when I saw him that last day. And later that night, after the storm, he went out to bury it. But the strain must have been too much for him. So he cut the work short, and headed back into the house. That's when he had the heart attack. That's why there was mud on his shoes."

"Yeah, but—"

"Wait, there's more. Over the past week I've noticed something strange. When the angle of the sun is just right, there's a glint in the garden at the side of the house."

"And you think it might be the mirror? But how, if it's buried?"

"Maybe it was harder work digging the hole than he thought. It was November by then, and the ground hadn't been worked in a long time. Besides, he was digging with a bad leg. Maybe he didn't get as deep as he would have liked. But he put the mirror in anyway and covered it up as well as he could. Maybe he was planning to come back and complete the job later, but he never got the chance.

"Then the cold weather set in, and the snow came and covered it over. But now that spring's come and we've had a few rains, it might have uncovered the mirror just enough that a tiny bit of it could reflect the rays of the sun."

"It's an interesting theory, Simon, but you know as well as I that the glint you're seeing could be caused by just about anything—a piece of glass from the window that broke when he fell, a bit of tin foil that blew into the yard. Any number of things."

As they were talking, a ball came bouncing their way across the grass. Abbey stuck out her foot to stop it. The small dog Simon had seen came bounding after it, yapping up a storm and wagging its tail wildly as it ran in circles around them. Its master was not far behind, a thin, fair-haired woman in large, dark sunglasses with a scarf tied around her hair.

"That's enough, Caesar. You just calm down now, you hear?" She was out of breath from running after the dog. "Sit," she said, panting, as she pushed her sunglasses back in place.

The dog sat, its large bright eyes darting back and forth between her and the ball, its tail thumping against the grass. It had a narrow head and long pointed ears that stood straight up from its head. Simon looked at it intently.

"Forgive me," said the woman. "He's just a pup. He gets a little rambunctious at times. Don't you, Caesar?" Caesar barked in reply.

"Will he bite?" asked Abbey.

"No. He's all yap and not much else."

"You're a little cutie, aren't you?" said Abbey. She bent down and stroked the puppy's head. "Caesar—such a big name for such a little dog."

"Oh, he'll get a lot bigger. He comes from an ancient line of hunting dogs. He'll be up to here in no time." And she held her hand waist-high off the ground.

"Are you going to be a big old hunting dog when you grow up?" said Abbey. The little dog barked and wagged its tail.

"Looks like you've made a friend," said the woman. She reached down and picked up the ball. "Come along now, Caesar. We've disturbed these young people quite enough for today. It was nice chatting with you," she said to Abbey, and then gave a brief nod to Simon—who hadn't said a word.

"You know, you weren't exactly Mr. Friendly, Simon," said Abbey.

But he was too busy watching the woman tramp off across the park to pay attention. There was something about her that sent chills through him. All the time she'd stood there at the bench, he felt her studying them intently with her eyes behind her dark glasses. He couldn't shake the feeling that it was more than mere coincidence that had sent the ball their way.

"What do you suppose she meant when she said she'd disturbed us enough *for today*. Why 'for today'?"

"It was just something to say, Simon. She was trying to be friendly—which was totally wasted on you, by the way."

The woman was over on the far side of the park now. As he watched she turned and glanced their way. No smile, no nod. Just a long steady look.

"Let's get going," he said. He stood up and started walking.

"Okay. I thought we were still talking—but I guess *not*." She shouldered her backpack and started after him, dumping the empty pop cans in a nearby bin.

He made a beeline for a side street that bordered the park. As they came to the sidewalk he glanced back over his shoulder. There was no sign of the woman and her dog. It was as if the ground had opened under them.

They walked along silently awhile.

"Did anyone ever mention paranoia as one of the symptoms of your illness, Simon? Pretty soon you're going to start suspecting Max and me."

"I'm going over there one night to check it out," he said.

"Over where? To the Hawkins house? Are you crazy? That's *trespassing*."

"There may not be another chance," he said. "Once they've moved in, it'll be too late. Are you in, or not?"

"Simon, *listen* to yourself. This is craziness."

He didn't say a word. He just stared down at his feet as they moved silently along the street. Slipper, shoe, slipper, shoe. How he hadn't noticed it before was a mystery.

"All right. All *right*," she said, when she couldn't stand it anymore. "I said I believed you. I promised I'd help. I'm in, okay? I'm in—Lord help me."

20

The new people's visits had become increasingly unpredictable. They could show up anytime during the evening. Sometimes, they'd stay for just a few minutes; at other times, they'd settle in for an hour or two. The one thing for certain was that once they left, they didn't return again that day.

Simon decided that the best time for him and Abbey to carry out their plan would be shortly after they'd left one night. Since that might be as late as midnight, Abbey insisted it be on a weekend.

While they waited for their opportunity, Simon put together the supplies they'd need. He found a couple of old gardening trowels hanging on the wall in the garage among his Granddad's tools, and an old canvas rucksack to carry them in.

He thought about bringing a flashlight, but some neighbor might notice the light and call the police. Since the glow from the streetlamps was too weak to illuminate the yard, they would have to wait for a clear night and rely on the moon for light. Meanwhile, there was nothing to do but wait.

The first weekend was gray and rainy. Apart from the want of a moon, it wouldn't do for them to be out digging in the mud. There was always a chance that either of them might be caught creeping back into their house afterwards. And muddy clothes would certainly give the game away.

He grew increasingly anxious with each passing day. It was just a question of time before the new people moved in. He spent his evenings awaiting their arrival, then stationed himself at the window and watched to see if anything they were doing might offer a clue to how close they were.

The woman walked in front in her regal way, while the man tagged along behind. They brought brooms and dustpans with them, mops and pails and cleaning supplies. It was clear they were readying the house for the move.

The following weekend the weather was clear and the moon was full. Abbey agreed it was now or never. They settled on Saturday night. That afternoon, with time heavy on their hands, they met at the park with Babs and Max. The kids came in their bathing suits and splashed in the pool. He and Abbey shed their shoes and waded barefoot round the rim, watching them. They bought soft serve cones from an ice-cream truck for everyone. The afternoon flew by without a hint of a cloud in the clear blue sky. There wasn't a word between them about what lay ahead that night, until they were saying their goodbyes.

"Say bye-bye to Max, Babs," said Simon. Babs pulled her hand free of his and ran over to Max. She planted a big sticky kiss on his cheek.

Max looked up at Abbey.

"Wasn't that nice?" she said. "Do you want to give Babs a good-bye kiss?"

He ran over and gave Babs a kiss back, then turned and started running off through the park.

"Bye, Babs," said Abbey, chucking her chin. Turning to Simon, she brought the first cloud of the day. "You're sure about tonight?" she said.

"Surer than I've ever been."

She made a brave stab at a smile. "I'll be waiting for your call," she said and started after Max.

Simon took Babs' sticky hand in his and clung tight to it all the way home.

It was after eleven when he made the call. The new people had been at the house a little more than an hour, and had just left. Abbey answered on the first ring.

"Is that you, Simon?" she whispered into the phone. "Look, my folks were out and just got home. I'll come as soon as they're settled."

"Wrong number," he heard her say as she hung up.

He pulled the knapsack out from under his bed and stationed himself at the window to wait. He could hear Babs turning in her sleep in the next room. He prayed she wouldn't wake up with a bad dream tonight of all nights and disturb Mom and Dad, who were already safely tucked in for the night.

Twenty minutes crawled by. Drifts of cloud sailed the night sky, periodically obscuring the moon, turning the

night pitch dark. He was hanging his head out the open
window, nervously scanning the sky, when a dark car drew
quietly up to the curb in front of the Hawkins house. He
ducked back inside and dropped down below the window.
They had come *back*!

For a long minute there was absolute silence. Then he
heard the light click of the car door opening. Peeking out
the window, he saw the man sprint up the porch steps and
head back into the house.

He crept to the far corner of the window and looked
down the street as far as he could see. There was still
no sign of Abbey, but any moment now she might come
strolling out of the gloom into the glow of the streetlights.

As he looked back at the old house a light came on
upstairs in the study. It spilled down into the yard, etching
a pattern of windowpanes on the grass, as though a light
had gone on underground. He saw a lean shadow flit there
as the man moved about the room.

Tearing his eyes away, he looked down the block
again—just as Abbey appeared in one of the pools of light
strung like pearls along the street. She was still too far off
for him to warn her. Along she came, casting her shadow
before her and reeling it in as she passed from one pool
to the next.

She would expect him to be out waiting by the bushes
in front of his house as they'd arranged. As she neared the
house, she noticed he wasn't there. He could sense her
confusion as she suddenly slackened her pace and hung
back in the shadows, wondering what was wrong.

Look up, he willed with all his might.

Across the street, the windows in the grass went dark as the lights in the study went out. Abbey started walking slowly toward Simon's house again. When she reached the lane, she turned and looked down it, checking to see if he might be there. He quickly poked his head out the window.

"Abbey," he whispered, as loud as he dared.

She looked up.

"Get *down*," he said with a desperate downward motion of his hand, and had time to see her duck behind a bush by the entrance to the lane just as the front door of the Hawkins house swung open, and the man came out carrying a box.

Simon yanked his head back inside and stepped to the side of the window, watching as the man hurried down the walk to the car, opened the passenger door, and put the box in. As he circled round to the driver's side he scanned the street up and down, then paused and took a long look down the lane. He started slowly across the road toward it. He got about halfway, when suddenly the tomcat with the torn ear burst from the shadows and raced down the street. The man followed it intently with his eyes, then turned and hurried toward the car. He slid in, started up the engine, and drove off down the street.

Abbey was still hiding behind the bushes when Simon stole out the window and down the trembling trellis a couple of minutes later.

"It's okay, Abbey," he whispered. "You can come out now."

"Was *that* the guy?" she asked, her eyes wide with alarm. Simon nodded.

"He's a little scary, Simon. No—a *lot* scary. Geez, I thought I'd die when he started walking my way. You said they were gone."

"They were. For some reason, he came back."

"You said they *never* came back."

"Yeah, well, this time he did. I'm sure he won't be back again."

"Yeah," she said, and took a long look down the street.

"You ready?" he said.

"Ready as I'll ever be."

Keeping to the shadows, they slipped down the street a ways and scooted across. Hunkering down beside parked cars, they approached the Hawkins house. On Simon's cue, they scurried up over the lawn. He reached up through the hole in the gate and felt for the catch. A moment later, they were in.

They squatted out of sight against the fence boards as they caught their breath and waited for their eyes to adjust to the dark. Pale shafts of light from the streetlamps seeped between the boards and died on the grass. A ghostly fleet of clouds sailed across the face of the moon. As they drifted off, the yard was bathed in sudden silver light.

"Over there," he said, pointing. "That bit of the garden below the window is where I saw the glint." Reaching into the rucksack, he took out the trowels. "I thought we'd be working together, but after what happened, maybe it's better to do it in shifts. One of us will stay here by the fence to keep an eye on the street, while the other digs. I've got a pretty good idea of where it is, so I'll go first."

"And what'll we do if I see the guy come back?"

"I don't know. Run, I guess."

"And just how far are *you* going to run, Simon?"

"He won't come back," he said after a pause.

"Yeah—but if he *does*?"

The old lilac bush where Simon had rooted around for the lost ball that day stood in the corner of the yard just inside the fence. It was in full flower now, the lush blooms luminous in the moonlight, the yard steeped in their scent.

"We can hide in there," he said, nodding toward it, "till he goes inside the house. Then we'll slip out."

Abbey looked doubtful. She turned and crept along the fence into the corner, disappearing into the deep shadows massed behind the bush. There was a long silence, then the fence quaked a little and he heard a faint creak. Abbey crept back.

"There's room there for both of us," she said. "I checked the fence boards. One of them was loose. I was able to push the bottom out with my foot. The gap's wide enough for us to squeeze through if we need to."

Another flotilla of clouds had drifted in, plunging them once again into darkness. Simon waited for it to clear, and then stole across the damp grass to the edge of the garden below the window. Squatting by the fence, Abbey pressed her eye to a gap between the boards. She gave the sign that all was clear, and he sank the trowel into the crusted soil.

It had all seemed so simple in his mind. The moon would be shining; they would slip in quickly, unearth the mirror he was sure lay buried there, and then steal easily away. It didn't seem so simple anymore. He dug around blindly in the dark as the clouds rolled in again. He'd been sure he knew the exact spot. But as the minutes passed, and he plunged the trowel repeatedly into the stubborn soil and struck nothing but dirt, he began to doubt.

Each time the clouds cleared and the moon showed its face, he looked hopefully for the telling glint he'd seen from across the street. But there was nothing. He glanced up at the window to get his bearings and gasped as a ghostly face peered back. But it was only the moon reflected in the glass.

His breath came short and sharp; his meager store of strength began to wane, and fatigue swept over him like a dark cloud. The trowel seemed pitifully small, the garden impossibly large. He had worked an area no more than four feet square, and had turned up only a few bits of broken glass, remnants from the window that crashed to the ground when Mr. Hawkins had his fall.

The whole mad plan seemed suddenly overwhelming. He sank back exhausted on his heels, sweat streaming down his face, and looked over at Abbey hunched up by the fence. He saw the concern on her face as she looked back and motioned him over.

"What is it, Simon?" she said as he sat down heavily beside her and leaned against the fence.

"I can't find it," he said, feeling breathless and faint. "It's not where I thought it would be. Perhaps we should just pack it in and leave. Maybe you were right, and the glint I saw was just from one of these." He opened his hand and showed her the shards of glass he had dug up, knowing even as he did that these dingy things could never have reflected the light he'd seen.

She read him like a book. "Not so fast, Simon," she said. "We're not leaving yet. Not after all this. You said this was our only chance, remember? Stay here and rest awhile, and I'll have a try. Where should I dig?"

"Try a little farther along," he said. "Closer to the house."

"Got it." She scooted across the grass, found a spot, and set to work.

Simon leaned against the fence and squinted through the gap at the dark, silent street. He heard a dull insistent thud in his ears and looked anxiously up and down the street for any sign of the car. But as the seconds passed and the street was still, he realized the thud he heard was the hammering of his heart.

The clouds sailed off, and the moon shone clear. In the soft, dreamlike light that washed the yard, he watched as Abbey probed the ground with the trowel, carefully turning the soil, working slowly toward the wall of the house. Finding nothing, she moved a little further along and began again. She worked steadily, without pausing to catch her breath or glance back at him.

He felt the light breeze on his face as it whispered through the gap in the fence, the damp grass against his legs. He looked across at his house, pictured Mom and Dad and Babs wrapped safely in sleep, while he and Abbey were abroad in the night, actors in this waking dream that had spun itself around the Hawkins house.

And then he heard it—an unmistakable metallic ring as Abbey's trowel struck something buried in the soil. He glanced over and saw her straighten up in surprise as she yanked out the trowel and looked back at him with wide, startled eyes.

In she went again, carefully now, feeling for the edge of whatever it was she'd struck. He watched her patiently clear away the soil, his excitement mounting till he could hardly contain himself. She laid the trowel aside and used her hands to brush the dirt away. Whatever it was lay shallow in the soil, close by the house, just past the window.

She sat back on her heels a moment, then reached in with both hands, and with one smooth motion, pulled the mirror free. It glimmered in the moonlight—a second moon held aloft in her hands. He heard a high faint cry, then realized with a shock it had come from him. Tears began to trickle down his cheek as some long-pent emotion was suddenly set free.

He scooted across the grass to her side. His hands shook as she handed him the mirror. He studied it back and front. It seemed unharmed by the long months spent under the ground. As he held it before him the bright face of the moon was mirrored in its depths.

Abbey carefully smoothed the soil where they'd been digging, patting it down with the flat of the trowel until it showed no signs of having been disturbed. She feathered the grass where they had knelt, erasing all traces of their presence there.

Simon tucked the trowels into the knapsack and slid the mirror in carefully alongside. They crouched by the fence and peered through the boards at the silent street.

"Are we going to put it in the garage?" she asked.

"No, I'm not letting it out of my sight."

"You're sure? Your folks are bound to see it and ask questions."

"Don't worry. I'll keep it safely hidden." He took one last look at the empty street. "Ready?"

She nodded her head.

Silent as shadows, they slipped from the yard and retraced their path up the street. They stood tucked in the shadows between streetlights.

"Try and get some rest, Simon. I'll come by as soon as I can."

"Thanks, Abbey. I'd never have found it without you."

"We're in this together, remember?" She looked one last time up and down the street. "Okay, I'm off," she said and scampered off into the night.

He watched till she was out of sight. Then he slipped across the road and along the street to his house. He clambered back up the trellis and through the open window without disturbing the sleepers, and silently readied himself for bed in the moon-washed room.

Loosening the neck of the knapsack, he slid the mirror out. It shone with an internal light. The sight of it woke a memory. He was looking at it lying on the table between him and Mr. Hawkins. He could almost see the old man sitting opposite him now, hear his voice sounding in the room.

He took the mirror and slid it under his mattress at the head of the bed. Crawling beneath the sheets, he closed his eyes and dropped almost instantly into a deep sleep. All night long, he crouched by the fence in the dream-lit yard, peering nervously through the gap for signs of the sleek black car.

21

On Monday, Abbey came by, math text in hand, to quiz Simon for the final exam next week.

"So where'd you hide it?" she asked as she closed his door quietly behind her.

He slid the mirror out from under the mattress.It was the first time Abbey had seen it in the light of day. She turned it back and front, buffed it on the sleeve of her shirt till it gleamed. She held it up in front of her and ran her eyes over it.

"It's beautiful," she said, "but I can't see anything magical about it."

"Sometimes it's there, and sometimes not," he said. There was dirt caked in the folds of the figure that formed the handle and the design of the eye incised on the face. She picked at it with her fingernail. As she went to hand the mirror back to him Simon caught sight of his reflection in its polished surface.

A figure peered one-eyed over his shoulder.

He whirled around—just as Abbey let go of the mirror, thinking he had it. It fell with a clang to the floor.

"Everything all right up there?" Mom called up the stairs.

"Just dropped a book," he said, scooping up the mirror and sliding it back under the mattress. There was a dint in the hardwood where the mirror had struck it edgewise. He slid the fringe of the rug over it as Mom's footsteps sounded on the stairs.

When she opened the door, they were sitting by the window, poring over the math text. "Would either of you like something to eat?" she asked. Her eyes darted around the room, looking for signs of damage.

"No, we're fine," they said, feigning innocence as they looked up from the book.

She made a point of leaving the door open behind her as she left the room. For a while they worked their way through the review exercises in the back of the book, Simon trying to coax his brain down paths it didn't want to take.

With the door open, it didn't take long before Babs wandered in with one of her puzzles. She dumped the pieces on the floor, flipped them right side up, and assembled them with lightning speed.

"You're really good at that, Babs," said Abbey.

"Don't encourage her," he warned. But it was already too late. In a matter of minutes, the floor was strewn with puzzle pieces, and the math review was a distant memory.

It was Babs who heard it first—a low rumbling noise outside that rattled the window. As she ran to look out, a large truck came creeping along the street and drew up to the curb in front of the Hawkins house. *Intercontinental*

Movers, read the writing on the side. *Long-distance Moving Specialists*.

"It's them," he said, a sick feeling in the pit of his stomach.

Three men in uniform with matching caps emerged from the cab of the truck and went around to the back. One of them unlocked the sliding door of the box trailer and shivered it open on its track. The others pulled out a metal ramp nesting under the box and banged the end of it down onto the road.

At that moment, a black car came drifting down the street and eased into the space in front of the moving van. The paint shone with a muted luster like the black stone mirror in Mr. Hawkins' collection, and the chrome trim gleamed in the sunlight. The door on the driver's side opened, and a woman in a broad-brimmed hat and sunglasses stepped out. A small copper-colored dog bounded out behind her.

Abbey's mouth fell open. "It's the woman from the park," she said. "Her hair's darker. But it's her, all right. That's the dog."

"Woo-woo," cried Babs and ran off to tell Mom.

It was the first time Simon had seen the new neighbor in the light of day. He'd had a strange feeling about the woman in the park, but he hadn't realized it was her. She walked over and spoke with the movers. The dog scampered along at her heels as she started up the walk to the house. It had grown since the day they saw it at the park.

The woman tied the dog to the fence and went up the stairs onto the porch. She opened the door for the movers, then went and sat down on the porch swing. With a light push of her foot against the floor, she set the swing in a shallow arc. Taking her hat off, she set it down on the seat beside her and primped her hair with the palm of her hand.

She had the studied air of one aware they were being watched. As indeed she was; all up and down the sleepy street—through lightly lifted blinds, discreetly parted curtains, the gauzy stealth of sheers—she was the object of a host of hungry eyes.

Already the news was racing through the slack wires slung from house to house. The phone hadn't stopped ringing since the moving van turned onto the street. Even Joe and the gang had stopped their game to gawk.

All pretense of studying laid aside, Simon and Abbey gazed transfixed as the movers trundled the new people's belongings down the shuddering ramp. There was not a great deal of furniture, but what there was was fine and rare. Swaddled in padded blankets, it was set down briefly on the lawn and unveiled to reveal the rich luster of antique things, and then eased gently up the stairs and through the door of the old house. And all the while the woman sat toeing the porch swing back and forth, directing where each piece was to go as it was carried past.

The younger children in the neighborhood ventured timidly near, inching up across the lawn to where the dog frisked about on its leash outside the fence. The woman smiled and said it was fine if they played with him, but they must be gentle. Soon, half a dozen of them were gathered on the lawn that had always been off-limits when the old man lived there.

Piece after piece, box after box, the new neighbors' belongings were carried smoothly into the old house. Only once, near the end, did the movers show signs of exertion as they labored a heavy item, shrouded in blankets and strapped to a dolly, down the buckling ramp and up the walk onto the lawn. Uncovered, it proved to be an old upright piano, the case elaborately carved and inlaid. A matching bench soon joined it on the lawn.

While the movers secured the wobbly porch stair with hammer and nails, and worked the stubborn pins from the hinges of the front door so that it could be removed to allow the piano to fit through, the woman drifted down from the porch and sat down at the piano. She tapped tentatively at the keys to see if it was still in tune, and then started to play a strange, haunting melody. The children sat spellbound on the lawn, listening.

The sound resonated through the street. It was as if the sky had stooped down and become a domed ceiling enclosing it, and the watchers at their windows were concertgoers tucked in their shadowed boxes in a hushed hall.

The music was moving and sad. She drew such feeling from the instrument that it was as if she sang through it. All else faded, and there was only the music. It was impossible to say how long she played, for she opened a door onto a realm where time no longer existed.

Then suddenly she stopped, and the spell lifted, and the sky leapt up again. Under her watchful eye, the movers wheeled the old piano slowly up the walk to the porch and eased it, step by cautious step, up the stairs and through the gaping doorway of the old house.

And she was in.

22

"And the cutest little dog," said Mom at the dinner table the next night. She'd baked some brownies as a housewarming gift and dropped them by at the new neighbors' earlier that day with Babs.

"She was *very* grateful, apologized for not inviting us in. She said the place was 'a total disaster.' She's very good with children—though she has none of her own. Made a big fuss over Babs. Let her pet the little dog. What was its name?"

"Caesar," muttered Simon.

"Ceasar—that's it," said Mom. "*Theirs* is Loudon. Alice and James. She's very nice. Well-spoken, refined. Fortyish, I'd say. Pretty—put together just so. Beautiful hands— long slender fingers. A concert pianist at one time, apparently. I'm not at all surprised, after hearing her play.

"She said she'd pop by for a visit once they were settled. I still haven't seen her husband. He was tying up some loose ends at their last place, she said. They've lived abroad for many years, and only recently moved back. Just happened to see the trustee's notice in the paper, she said. Babs, honey, use your *fork*, not your *fingers*."

Babs brandished the fork in her fist while she scooped up the last of the mac and cheese with the other hand. "More," she said, holding out the empty bowl. Mom went to get her a second helping.

"How are they related to the Hawkins?" asked Dad.

"Eleanor's niece, I gather. The only child of Eleanor's older sister, Daphne. Eleanor and she never quite saw eye to eye, from what Eleanor said. She was too much the bohemian for Daphne's tastes, and Daphne too much the social climber for hers. She married into money and moved east. Died a few years before Eleanor. It's funny, though; I don't remember Eleanor mentioning a niece.

"Anyway, it's nice the Loudons have turned up. So much better that the house stay in the family. They plan to spruce it up and settle in. It could have been *so* much worse. I'd begun to worry that someone might bulldoze the old place. Frankly, I'm relieved."

Simon wished he could feel relieved. But as the Loudons slowly began to weave their spell over the neighborhood, all he could feel was a keen sense of dread.

No sooner did James Loudon appear on the scene a few days later, than he was outside the house with hammer and nails and saw, busily mending the many things Mr. Hawkins had let slide. He replaced the damaged tread on the porch steps, the missing slats in the rail, and the loose board in the old fence, which flapped in the wind. He pried up the sagging planks in the porch floor and laid down new ones, planed the edge of the front door till it opened with scarcely a whisper.

He righted the old mailbox that had dangled from one screw for so long that it was simply part of the house, cut back the wisteria branch that had come down in the storm, and scaled the rickety wooden ladder to seal the hole in the gable roof where the squirrels had gotten in. He scraped the loose paint from the eaves trough and trim. The flakes flurried down like summer snow on the overgrown garden.

Day after day, dawn to dusk, he worked—with barely a break. He was more machine than man. Sitting by the window with his math book, Simon marveled at his strength, his boundless store of energy, the effortless ease with which he moved.

"Okay, Simon, you have forty-five minutes," said Abbey as she handed him the math test. She checked her watch. "Starting...now."

Miss Court had entrusted her with overseeing the test, and she took zealously to the task. As on the other tests she'd supervised, she offered him no hints—no help of any kind. She became a miniature Miss Court, down to adopting her mannerisms as she sat with legs crossed, twirling her foot, till he finally asked her to stop.

With the prep work done, the Loudons had begun to repaint the outside of the old house. Alice Loudon, in a pair of old jeans and a loose shirt knotted at the waist, was working on the porch railing. James Loudon scrambled spiderlike up the steep ladder to the highest reaches of the house to paint the gable and the eaves trough.

Simon saw a look of awe steal into Abbey's eyes as she watched. She gave him a look.

"I can hear you thinking, Simon. And you're wrong. So relax, will you? I'm not going over to the dark side. Promise." She looked down at the empty page and glanced at her watch. "Thirty minutes now."

But without her help to constantly prod him along, he was hopelessly lost. He bombed the test. It was summer school now for sure.

With the painting complete, the old place was transformed from the eyesore it threatened to become to the jewel of the neighborhood it had been in its prime. The lilac in the yard was pruned, the bushes trimmed and shaped, the lawn cut and edged, the soil in the garden topped and turned. A new striped awning graced the porch swing. The flowerbed that fronted the porch was cleared of its weeds. Daisies and daylilies took their place.

Neighbors slowed as they passed, astonished at the change.

"I can hardly believe it," said Mom as she stood at the living-room window looking over at the house. "It's like a dream."

23

The battered blue dumpster gouged deep furrows in the Loudon's lawn as it was lowered into place. Over the following days it began to fill up. From his vantage point Simon had a clear view down into it.

Several pieces of the Hawkins' furniture were the first to go, among them the armchairs from the front room, their upholstery slit, their stuffing and springs exposed. Soon they were buried beneath boxes of broken plaster and lath, and splintered lengths of wainscoting stripped from the upstairs walls.

Many a night, he woke with a start to the creak and crack of boards, the groan of heavy objects being dragged about, and crept to the open window to the find the lights burning in the old house, and the couple's shadows flitting like ghosts upon the curtains.

The neighbors doubtless believed it was simply the Loudons working as tirelessly to whip the inside of the old house into shape as they had the outside. But Simon was convinced it was more.

They were hunting for the mirror. He was *sure* of it. There was something more than human about the relentlessness of their search. He knew it would continue day and night, for as long as it took, until they found what they were after. They would *never* grow tired; they would *never* give up.

It wore on him to be right across the street from them, the first house they saw when they looked out. So far he was safe, but it couldn't last. It was simply a matter of time before they learned of his connection with Mr. Hawkins and the house. He dreamed of escape. If he had his strength back he would run, he told himself. But where could he run to that he would not have to return from? And when he did, they would be here, waiting.

He woke one morning to find the mirror in bed beside him, lying face down among the rumpled sheets like another sleeper. He had no memory of having taken it out. He leapt out of bed, slid it safely out of sight under the mattress, smoothed the sheets, and drew the bedspread up over all. He watched in the mirror as his double dressed and ran a brush through his hair.

Padding down the hall to the bathroom, he peeked through Babs' bedroom door. Random cushions were laid out on the floor in front of her crib like puzzle pieces. Two nights ago, the inevitable had finally occurred; she'd gone over the rail.

The thud of her fall had jarred him from sleep. He was first to her room and found her sitting on the floor, crying. It wasn't simply a hurt cry, but one of shock and indignation. She'd spent months trying to master the art of escaping the crib. Now finally she'd done it. And *this* was her reward?

He scooped her up in his arms and tried to comfort her. Mom came running up the stairs. A lump had already ballooned up on Babs' forehead. Mom went to fetch some ice to bring down the swelling, and some baby aspirin to help calm her. For the remainder of the night, they woke her every hour and peered into her eyes with a penlight to make sure she was all right.

He heard voices drifting up the stairs now as he started down. One was Mom's. He couldn't place the other, though he was sure he'd heard it before.

Babs ran to meet him. The bump on her forehead had begun to come down, but the deep bruise showed through her bangs, and if you went anywhere near it, she screamed blue murder.

"Dimon, woo-woo," she said, tugging him toward the front room.

He felt the hairs rise on the back of his neck as he remembered where he'd heard that voice before.

Mom's back was to him as he came into the doorway of the room. She was perched on the edge of the couch, pouring tea from the pink teapot that normally sat untouched on the top shelf of the china cupboard. She had also taken down two delicately fluted cups and matching saucers.

The object of this fuss sat in the chair across from her. It was Alice Loudon. She wore a long-sleeved linen dress, set off with a pearl necklace and matching earrings. She looked out of place, as if she'd wandered into the wrong neighborhood by mistake. Lying placidly at her feet, its head resting on its paws, was the little dog.

She looked up at him over the rim of her cup as she brought it to her mouth, fixing him with a long, level gaze. It was the first time he'd seen her without her sunglasses. Though very striking with her finely tooled features and large dark eyes, she was older than he'd imagined. Beneath the heavy makeup she wore, the web of fine lines around her eyes and mouth betrayed her age.

The dog, too, had noticed him. Suddenly it rose up—no longer the playful pup he had seen in the yard, but something primitive and fierce. The muscles tensed like cables under its fur, and fire flared in its eyes. It let out a low threatening growl. For a moment, it was the spitting image of the dog he'd seen in the Hawkins yard.

A look of curiosity came to Alice Loudon's face. Her hand fell to the dog's head. "Be still," she said. Instantly it lay down, again the pup that played on the lawn.

"Ah, Simon," said Mom. "I'm glad you came down. Our new neighbor has dropped by for a visit. I was just telling her how close you and her uncle had grown after his fall. Mrs. Loudon—my son, Simon."

"I believe Simon and I have met," she said.

"Oh?" said Mom.

"Yes, in a park not far from here—before we moved in. I was with Caesar. And you were with a young lady," she said, turning to Simon.

Mom cast him a questioning glance.

"I went to meet Abbey on her way home from school one day," he explained. "We stopped to talk in the park."

"She seemed like a very sweet girl," said Mrs. Loudon.

"Yes, she is," agreed Mom. "She lives in the neighborhood, goes to the same school as Simon. She and Simon have been seeing quite a bit of one another recently, haven't you, Simon?"

"Yes," he said, wishing desperately she would stop.

"You're embarrassing the poor boy," said Mrs. Loudon with a smile.

Babs took him by the hand and drew him into the room, sitting him down on the end of the couch. She scooped two cookies from the plate Mom had put out, handed him one, then scrambled up onto his lap and perched there, swinging her legs back and forth.

"Woo-woo," she said, craning her neck to look up into Simon's face. Noticing Mrs. Loudon looking her way, she fell back against his chest and tucked her face under his arm. He tried to urge her out, but she was wedged in tight.

"How sweet," said Mrs. Loudon as Babs peeked out at her.

"Please have a cookie," said Mom, holding out the plate. "I just baked them this morning. They're Babs' favorite— as you can probably gather."

The guest took one and perched it on the edge of her saucer.

"Now, what were we talking about?" said Mom. "Ah, yes—Abbey. She's been a godsend for Simon—for all of us, actually. Simon's been sick for the past few months and unable to go to school. Abbey's been tutoring him. Thanks in large part to her, it looks like he'll get his year."

"Sick?" said Mrs. Loudon. "May I ask what's been wrong?"

"I wish we could say. It's been something of a mystery, I'm afraid. Fever, sore throat, swollen glands—and an incredible fatigue along with it. He was sleeping *eighteen* hours a day, at its worst. He could barely walk from one side of his room to the other. The weeks went by, and it got no better."

Simon felt Mrs. Loudon's gaze drift over him like a chill wind as she looked him up and down.

"We went the round of doctors, had countless tests done, but we were still no nearer to discovering what it could be. The best guess seems to be that it's some phantom virus. With plenty of rest and no undue stress, the doctors assure us he'll recover. It's been slow, but we're beginning to see some improvement, aren't we, Simon?"

He gave her a look that said, *Please stop.*

"I'm sorry," said Mom. "I'm talking too much."

"Nonsense," said Mrs. Loudon. "I suffer from a chronic illness myself. I know the frustration of not feeling well, of suddenly being unable to do things you once could, of losing yourself little by little to illness."

Simon was taken aback by the unveiled emotion in her voice.

"I've found that certain traditional remedies have been a great help to me," she went on. "I could put something together for you, if you'd like. It will certainly do you no harm, and it could well do some good."

"We wouldn't want to trouble you," said Mom.

"No trouble at all. I'd be pleased to help in whatever way I could. After all, we sick folk must stick together." She cast a look Simon's way. It was unreadable—as was everything about her. He looked into her eyes, then quickly looked away, his head whirling. It was like peering down into a dark pool. He clutched Babs close, till she squirmed to be let go.

"You've done wonders with the house," said Mom as Babs scrambled up onto her lap with another cookie in hand. "It looks like it did when I was a child."

"You're very kind. Have you lived on the street all your life, then?"

"This was my family's home when I was growing up," Mom explained. "I moved away when I got married, then recently moved back, after my dad died."

"It's charming," said Mrs. Loudon, sweeping her eyes around the modest room. "I'm afraid our place is still in rather a state. I seem to be constantly looking for things I can't seem to lay my hands on."

Simon stole a look her way, but she failed to meet it.

"I'm sure you'll sort it out in no time," said Mom. "It must be hard going through all the family things."

"Yes, but it needs to be done," she said with seeming sincerity—as Simon thought about the boxes tossed unceremoniously in the trash.

"Your aunt and uncle were a dear couple," said Mom. "Did you get to see them much?" She was probing. Mrs. Loudon sensed it and instantly stiffened.

"Not often enough, I'm afraid. Family get-togethers over the years. Cards and letters. The last time I saw them was at my mother's funeral." She was clearly uncomfortable with the turn the conversation had taken.

Simon saw a look flit across Mom's face as she ran her fingers through Babs' hair, inadvertently uncovering the bump on her forehead. Babs recoiled.

"Oh, that's a nasty-looking bump," said Mrs. Loudon.

"Yes, *someone* has discovered how to escape her crib."

"I see," said Mrs. Loudon. She reached for her purse. Taking out a small compact, she studied her face in the mirror, turning from side to side. It was a simple gesture, but to Simon it seemed she laid hold of her reflection like a drowning person latches onto a piece of wreckage. He watched intently as she powdered a spot high on her right cheek. A thin red line showed momentarily through the make-up.

Closing the compact with a click, she slipped it back into her purse and came out holding what looked to be a business card. "I wonder if I might leave this with you," she said, passing it to Simon.

Over a pale pen-and-ink drawing of a piano, the words

ALICE LOUDON
Piano Instruction
Reasonable rates - All Ages

were embossed in an antique type. He passed it to Mom.

"Ah, so you teach," she said.

"For a good many years now—since I stopped performing. I don't know what I'd do without it. It gives me life. I see you have a piano. Do you play?"

"A little," said Mom. "The piano was my dad's. He loved

to play. Simon learned to play on his knee. *He* plays very well, even took lessons for a little while, though he hasn't shown much interest lately."

"Well, it's never too late," said Mrs. Loudon.

She rose and walked toward the piano. As she passed the full-length mirror in its wooden frame, she fixed on her reflection.

"May I?" she asked. Reaching down, she danced her fingers over the keys. "It has a nice tone. They don't make pianos like this these days. Mine's an old Bechstein. I've been playing it for years. It goes wherever I go."

She played a few bars of the piece set out on the stand. She coaxed a magic from the keys. The old piano had never sounded so good. "Lovely," she said. "You know, I have some old sheet music at home you might like—if I can find it."

The dog rose and walked alongside her as she moved toward the door. Mom followed with Babs on her hip. Babs' eyes were riveted on the dog as its claws clacked against the bare floor.

"You've been *most* kind," said Mrs. Loudon, putting her sunglasses back on. "Thank you very much for the tea. It was good to see you again, Simon. I'll drop by that medicine I mentioned."

"Seems very nice, doesn't she?" said Mom as she closed the door behind her and put Babs down. The moment she was down, Babs made a beeline for the living room. Mom hurried after her and whisked the cookie plate out of reach. She began gathering up the cups and saucers.

"Odd," she said. "She didn't touch her tea or cookie."

He could tell there was something more on her mind, and asked what it was.

"Oh, it's silly. Just something she said about her mother's funeral. She said she'd seen the Hawkins there. But I seem to recall that Eleanor went alone. Randall was away on a dig somewhere. I'm sure it's nothing."

24

He was jarred awake by a loud bang. A large truck had tethered heavy chains to the dumpster on the Loudon's lawn and was hauling it up onto its back. The bin was so full that the driver had to tie a tarp down over it so that the stuff wouldn't blow off.

He was home alone later that afternoon when the front doorbell rang. Abbey had said she'd drop by with the math syllabus for summer school. He ran to get it, eager to tell her about Alice Loudon's visit. But when he opened the door, Alice Loudon was standing there.

"Hello, Simon," she said pleasantly, peering at him through her dark glasses. "I brought you the medicine I was telling you about." She reached into her bag and pulled out a piece of paper folded into a little packet.

"Take a spoonful of this and pour boiling water over it to make a tea," she said, handing it to him. "Drink it once a day. It's a bit bitter, but don't mind the taste. It will do you good, if you keep it up."

"Thank you," he said.

"You're most welcome. Is your mother in, by any chance?"

"No, she's at work." He held the door close against him in case she had any notion of coming in.

"I see. Well, I found that music I was telling her about." She pulled a sheaf of sheet music from her bag and handed it to him. "Perhaps you could pass this along to her for me."

Hooking the bag onto her shoulder, she turned to go.

"Oh, one more thing," she said, turning back. "Your mother mentioned you'd become quite close to my uncle."

Simon felt like he'd been punched in the stomach. "Yes," he said. "I took dinner over to him sometimes, after he broke his leg."

"I was wondering if you might have noticed a little mirror he had. It was a family heirloom, you see, and I was hoping I'd find it among his things. But I can't seem to lay my hands on it. It's a small bronze mirror, slightly elliptical in shape—like a flattened circle." She made the shape with her hands. "There's an eye engraved on one side. And the handle takes the form of the goddess Beset—a woman with the head of a lion." There was a stifled urgency in her tone.

"That sounds like the mirror that hung in the front room across from his chair," he said. "Isn't it there still?" He tried to keep his voice calm and measured as he gripped the door.

"I'm afraid not. And you have no idea what might have happened to it?"

"No. I'm sorry, I don't." He felt himself trembling from head to toe.

"Ah, well, it will turn up, I suppose. After all—where could it have gone? Tell your mother I hope she likes that music. And be sure to take that tea. You'll be as good as new again in no time. Who knows, we may even persuade you to take up the piano again. And should you happen to remember anything more about that mirror—anything at all, mind—you will let me know, won't you? I'm most anxious to find it."

As she started down the walk he closed the door and stood with his back against it, the blood thundering in his ears. The conversation kept looping 'round and 'round in his mind. Had he said anything that might make her think he was lying? Had his face somehow betrayed him?

He was so caught up in his thoughts that he failed to hear the light tread of footsteps on the porch stairs. The knocker came down like a hammer blow against his back, and he realized with a shock that she'd come back.

More knocks followed—harder now. She knew he was home. If he didn't answer, she'd be sure to suspect something. Steeling himself, he opened the door.

"Abbey—you scared me half to death." Whisking her into the house, he bolted the door behind them.

"What's going on, Simon?"

"Alice Loudon was just here. I thought you were her, coming back."

"What did she want?"

"She brought me this," he said, handing her the paper packet. He told her about Alice Loudon's visit to the house the night before, his glimpse of the scar on her cheek, his mom telling her about his sickness, and her offer to bring him some traditional medicine she prepared.

"My mom told her about my taking dinner to Mr. Hawkins, and how close we'd become," he said. "So when she showed up with the medicine, she asked me about the mirror. She kept on about whether I was sure I didn't know what had happened to it. She suspects something, Abbey. I know she does. What am I going to do?" His breath came short and sharp.

"The first thing you're going to do is lie down before you fall down," she said. She helped him up the stairs to his room. Fear had flung him back into the abyss of illness. Climbing the short flight of stairs felt like scaling Mount Everest.

"Just lie there and rest awhile," she said as he flopped across the bed. Taking the packet, she wandered over to the light of the window to look at it.

"What are you supposed to do with this?" she asked as she carefully unfolded the paper.

"I'm supposed to make a tea. She says it'll help restore my strength."

"Lord, it smells like *death*," said Abbey, recoiling as she took a sniff. Nipping a pinch of the pungent brown powder, she took a tentative taste. "*Eww*—you're supposed to *drink* this stuff? It's disgusting, Simon."

She held it out for him to take a sniff. The smell made his stomach lurch. She refolded the packet and put it on the bedside table.

"What's this?" she said, picking up the little card that lay there.

"She left it last night. It's her business card. She teaches piano."

"I'm not surprised, having heard her play." She laid it back down. "Now tell me exactly what she said about the mirror."

"She said it was a family heirloom. She was hoping to find it among Mr. Hawkins' things, but couldn't. She knew I'd become friends with him, so she asked me if I'd seen it. She described it in exact detail. She said that the figure on the handle was the goddess Beset. She even knew about the eye. I told her I'd seen a mirror like it, hanging on Mr. Hawkins' living room wall. But if it wasn't there now, I had no idea where it had gone. I'm not sure she believed me."

Abbey stood looking out the window. "Simon," she said suddenly, "I think I just saw your new neighbor going into a house down the street."

Ten minutes later, they watched as Alice Loudon emerged from the Glovers' house and moved on to the Pimentels' next door.

"What she's up to? I wonder," Simon said.

That night, at the dinner table, the mystery was explained. Several neighbors on the street had called Mom to say Alice Loudon had dropped by that day to introduce herself and leave one of her cards with them. They went on about how charming she was, what fine jewelry she wore, the cut and quality of her clothes. They seemed awed to have been caught up in her orbit, like commoners who have had a brush with royalty.

By the end of the week, two children on the street had been signed up for piano lessons. As the fires of competition were fanned, more followed. Soon, half the children on the street were signed up—along with a smattering of adults eager to get a peek inside the house. The baseball game languished for want of players, as many in the gang that had gathered around Joe Pimentel drifted off.

Over the next month, three reconditioned uprights were delivered on the street. When the Bouchards had their piano tuned, Simon's mother made arrangements for the tuner to come by and tune theirs as well. Alice Loudon's sheet music was set out on the stand. The halting strains of Mom's playing stumbled up the stairs to Simon's room.

Culture had come to the quiet little street, and the hub of it was the Loudon house. As summer settled in, a steady stream of children passed silent as shadows along the street, piano books tucked under their arms, and disappeared through the door of the Loudon house.

With the weather hot and the windows open, the sounds of scales and exercise pieces drifted to Simon's ears throughout the day. And late at night, as he drifted off to sleep, the last thing he often heard was the faint, haunting sound of her playing.

Despite Mom's repeated urgings that he sign up, he resisted the seduction—as he resisted the contents of the little paper packets periodically delivered to his door. Abbey was right. They smelled like death.

25

The more the neighborhood fell under the Loudons' spell, the more uncomfortable Simon became. Even Mom, who had initially been troubled by some of Alice Loudon's memories of the Hawkins, seemed to cast all doubts aside after she decided to sign up for lessons herself. But as he pondered what she'd said about Eleanor Hawkins having never mentioned a niece, his thoughts went to the trove of photo albums in the garage.

The albums he'd discovered in the boxes had been mostly devoted to their travels to remote archaeological sites around the world, where Mr. Hawkins' work had taken him. But there was another album—the album of family photos he'd searched through that first day he brought dinner to the old man; the one with the photo of the two boys on the porch steps. He could picture it clearly with its blue binding, but he couldn't remember having seen it in the box with the others—or in any of the other boxes he'd gone through.

Had he overlooked it somehow? The prospect of rooting through the boxes again was overwhelming. The sense of dread that had settled on him since Alice Loudon turned her attention his way had erased the slow gains he'd made in his recovery. The debilitating fatigue was back again, draining his strength and fogging his brain. It was another steep, sudden plunge of the roller coaster he'd been riding since illness struck. He kept thinking the ride was coming to an end, only to find the bottom suddenly fall out again.

With Mom at work and Babs at Mrs. Pimentel's, he was alone in the house most afternoons. Abbey and he had taken to meeting for an hour or so a day at the picnic table out back to try to batter some math into his head before summer school began.

"Isn't this the woman you said was a friend of Mr. Hawkins?" she said as she handed him the newspaper she'd brought with her one afternoon. Joan Cameron peered up at him from the folded paper.

"That's her, all right." She was a few years younger in the picture, but there was the same quiet intensity in her gaze. The photo accompanied an article headed, *Mysterious Theft at Museum*:

> *Over the past several months the Caledon Museum has fallen victim to two mysterious thefts. Dr. Joan Cameron, curator of the museum's Egyptology department, reports that in each instance it was display cases in the Egyptian gallery that were targeted. Last spring, a rare bronze snake wand went missing. And in recent weeks, an amuletic necklace of gold and semi-precious stones vanished from a case containing some of the earliest acquisitions in*

the museum's collection, part of the find discovered by Edmund Walker in the 1890s, which includes the museum's famous mummy. In neither instance was there any sign of tampering with the case.

Dr. Cameron urges any visitors to the museum over the past few weeks who may have noticed any unusual activity in the gallery to contact the police at once. "We are at a loss to explain how these priceless artifacts could have gone missing," she said. "It's as though they disappeared by magic."

"Strange, eh?" said Abbey.

"Yeah. Can I hang on to this?"

"Sure."

He told her about his plan to go through the boxes in the garage again in search of the missing photo album. Abbey offered to help.

On the night they'd rescued the boxes from the garbage, it had been far too dark to see much of anything inside the garage. So as he slipped the padlock off the hasp and opened the garage door the following afternoon, he turned to Abbey and warned, "It's a bit of a mess."

"A *bit*?" she said as her eyes fell on the mountain of junk massed on the dirt floor inside. "Where do we start?"

"With these over here," he said, pointing out two of the Hawkins' boxes tucked among his granddad's things. They hauled them out, wrestled a couple of wobbly wooden chairs from the chaos, and set to work.

"We're looking for an old photo album with a blue cover," he said as they flipped open the flaps of the boxes.

"Simon, *everything* in here is old," she said.

With the sun beating down on the tin roof, it was a sweatbox inside the garage. Sunlight streaked through gaps in the old boards that made up the walls. Outside, the boards had been painted, but here the bare wood was all splintery and splotched with damp. The dust storm they'd set off as they dug out the chairs churned in the shafts of light that sifted through the corrugated tin roof.

An hour went by. Now and then a car came bumping down the rutted lane, grinding the gravel beneath its wheels, pinging pebbles off the side of the garage as it went by. They pulled down all the boxes and went through them one by one, but failed to turn up the missing album. Tired and sweaty, they looked down bleakly at the boxes strewn round them on the floor.

"Wait," said Abbey suddenly. "We took two loads of four boxes in the wagon that night. There should be eight boxes here. There are only seven. One's missing."

They started rooting through the clutter again, looking for it. It was Simon who finally found it, tucked beneath the workbench on top of Granddad's old wooden tool chest. He had no memory of putting it there. The box was unmarked. It was not one of the ones he'd gone through.

They set it down on the floor between them and popped the flaps. Halfway down, buried beneath a pile of old gardening magazines scooped from the shelves in the Hawkins living room, they found the missing album.

As he started leafing through it Simon recalled the first time he'd gone through the album, under Mr. Hawkins' watchful eye. He came to the page with the blank space where the photo of the boys on the porch stairs had been. It was just one in a flurry of pictures taken that summer. On the following pages were others he hadn't seen that day, including two pages of photos taken inside the museum. One showed young Hawkins bending low to peer into the mummy case.

After that, there was only a smattering of photos from Hawkins' high school years, as the gangly boy grew into a handsome young man. The last of them, taken at the grad dance, showed him standing with his date. Beneath it, in her careful hand, Eleanor Hawkins had written, "First date."

After a break of two pages, the album started up again, now with Eleanor's family photos. Her father had been a stockyard worker, and they'd lived in a humble little house down near the tracks. There were no formal studio shots, just random snaps of the family as it grew. Dog-eared and wrinkled, they showed signs of having been stored haphazardly down the years, then rescued and consigned to the calm of the album. All were neatly labeled in Eleanor's hand.

There were two children in the family. Eleanor's sister, Daphne, was older—lean and long like her mother. Eleanor was short like her father. Daphne loved the camera, while Eleanor clearly did not. Daphne wore the latest fashions, while Eleanor dressed simply and starkly. By the time she was in her teens, there was already something of the bohemian about her.

After high school, the sisters went their separate ways—Daphne off to university, Eleanor to college in town. There was a shot of Daphne and her beau in their caps and gowns at graduation. And a wedding photo two years later, with Eleanor standing amidst the matching bridesmaids looking glum.

Then, Daphne with her newborn baby at the hospital. A photo from the christening—the baby in a long lace gown, the new mom and dad beaming as they held the child.

Then an ominously empty page, followed on the next by a prayer card with a picture of an angel leading a child by the hand over a little white bridge. Below it was an obituary notice clipped from the local paper:

> *Charles and Daphne Grosvenor are grieved to announce the death of their infant child, Alice Jane, age six months.*

Beneath the brittle notice Eleanor had written two stark words: "Crib death."

After that, the photos were few. Daphne and her husband posing for Christmas pictures down the years—graying, aging. Loss had left its stamp upon them—a guardedness about his eyes, grief tucked among the folds of her gown. Finally, a prayer card from the funeral of Daphne Grosvenor, with a photo of a young Daphne on the front, before death came to call.

"So sad," said Abbey.

"You see what this means though, don't you?" said Simon. "That baby who died is the niece Alice Loudon claims to be."

The wind chime hanging from the beam above them began to tinkle lightly in the hot, still air. Abbey put a finger to her lips and pointed toward the side of the garage skirting the lane. There was a faint scrabbling just on the other side of the wall, followed by a high, troubled whine. Then, the sound of footsteps approaching along the lane, and a light, eerie whistling. Simon recognized the tune as the one he'd heard Alice Loudon play a few nights before, and his blood froze.

A shadow passed slowly along the side the garage, quenching the light through the cracks, now here, now there. There was a sudden, frenzied scratching at the double doors of the garage, followed by loud, insistent barking.

"Stop that, Caesar." The voice was unmistakably Alice Loudon's. The dog whimpered and let out a flurry of stifled barks.

"Come away from there—now. There's nothing for you there."

The shadow passed and the dog scurried off. Simon and Abbey began to breathe again. As the sounds faded into the distance, they stole over to the double doors and put their eyes to the crack between them.

Alice Loudon was ambling off along the lane, with Caesar trailing behind. Even as they watched, the dog turned and took a lingering look their way.

26

All through July, the Loudons spent long hours in their yard, tending their garden and taking in the sun. Since the yard ran along the side of the house, much of their activity was on view to the neighbors. Simon was convinced this was no coincidence. Their actions increasingly appeared to him to be part of an elaborate performance.

To the casual observer they doubtless seemed the perfect couple, their lives like something clipped from the pages of a magazine. But no one watched them with the same attention that he did. They might glimpse them briefly from a window, see them for a moment as they passed by the house. He alone remained fixed at his perch hour after hour like an eagle in its aerie.

Illness had shaped him to see what others did not. He studied their body language, their gestures, the fleeting expressions that crossed their faces. Math problems, science concepts, even the simplest of words often eluded him in the fog that filled his brain. But here was a study perfectly suited to him, and he noted every nuance like a scholar.

"There's something strange about them," he said to Abbey. "The way they are with one another."

"How do you mean?"

"It's not so much what they do; it's what they don't. It's like they're *playing* at being affectionate. But in all the time I've watched them, I've never once seen him take her hand, give her a hug or a kiss, show any sign of warmth toward her. It's weird. My folks are far from being love-birds, but they laugh at one another's jokes, they touch, they kiss. I've never seen the Loudons do any of those things. That's what's strange."

Later that week, they were sitting at the window in his room. Across the street, the Loudons were out in their yard. They had set up a patio table on the lawn at the side of the house, shaded by a large, bright umbrella. She was sitting reading at the table. It was late afternoon. He was mixing drinks for them, as he often did at that time of day. He poured a shot of liquor into a glass, added a spritz of soda, dropped in two ice cubes with metal tongs, and then passed it to her.

As she glanced up from her book to take it from him, his hand happened to brush hers. She recoiled as if she'd been shocked. The glass fell to the grass, and a dark look flashed across her face as she sat bolt upright in her chair.

James Loudon stepped back, brought his hands up to his chest, and bobbed his head, before stooping to pick up the glass. The whole exchange lasted mere seconds, then all returned to normal. He remade the drink, but now he set it down on the table beside her.

"Did you *see* that?" said Abbey.

After that, Abbey's eyes were glued to everything they did. And she noticed something even stranger about them, something that was to prove a vital clue to who Alice Loudon really was.

"He makes this elaborate show of mixing her drink," she said as they were observing the ritual another day. "But have you ever actually seen her drink it?"

"I don't know."

"Watch," she said.

They watched Alice Loudon absently turn the glass on the table as she read. From time to time, she took it up in her hand and touched the cool glass to her cheek, then set it down again, untasted. Finally, she picked up the drink, held it down by her side, and discreetly emptied it onto the lawn.

"See," said Abbey. "It's the same when he makes her something to eat. He barbeques steaks, puts one on a plate and sets it down on the table in front her. She cuts it into small pieces, toys with it, but never eats a bite of it. Eventually, he wanders off into the house. A few minutes later, the dog comes running out and stations itself by her side. By then the steak is cold. She tips it onto the grass as if she were emptying scraps. And the dog gobbles it up.

"And that's another strange thing. The dog. You see it alone in the yard. You see it with her. But have you ever seen him and the dog together?"

"I'm sure I have."

"Well, I haven't—ever."

Caesar had grown alarmingly since the Loudons first moved in. He spent most evenings shut in the yard alone, ceaselessly prowling the property, ever on the alert for any small animals that might wander into his domain. It was then, as the dark fell and the shadows claimed him as their own, that he most reminded Simon of the dog he'd seen from the study window.

The squirrels that once ran wild in the Hawkins yard were strangely absent now. The birds had deserted the cedars, taking their songs with them. The cats that once crossed the yard on their way to and from the cat-lady's house next door now went a safer way. All save for one— the old tomcat with the torn ear.

Rather than slink down the alley with the others, he strutted along the top rail of the high fence that separated the yards, safely out of the dog's reach. From time to time, he'd pause to lick a paw and cast a disdainful glance down into the Loudon's yard, before leaping down on the opposite side to enjoy his dinner outside the cat-lady's door. All the while, the dog sat on its haunches, absolutely still, staring intently up at the cat.

The display went on for several weeks as Simon watched. Then one day, as the cat paused midway along the fence to scratch its ear, the dog struck. Without a hint of warning, it sprang from a sitting position high into the air, and plucked the cat off the rail like a ripe peach off a bough. There was one quick startled cry, cut short, as they dropped out of sight behind the bushes. Then silence. A long while later, the dog emerged...alone.

After that, the dog took to leaping the Loudons' fence many nights, prowling the street for strays of all sorts. More than once, Simon stole to the window in the night and found it stationed in front of the house, staring up at him.

27

Everyone assumed that when school started up again in the fall Simon would go. He'd been ill for months and missed the better part of a year of school. He'd passed through a period of blankness. But the worst of it was behind him now, and things would soon return to the way they'd been before he became sick.

Summer school would help ease him back into the swing of things, Mom said. It would just be for a month, and there'd only be the one subject to worry about. The daily trek to and from the school would help build up his strength. And since it was only for half a day, he'd be able to nap in the afternoon if he was tired. She was so gung ho about it, she left little room for doubt. How could he begin to tell her what he'd come increasingly to believe—that things would never again be as they'd been before?

No one wanted him to be well more than he did himself, but all the wanting in the world couldn't change the way he felt. It was one thing to tinker around the house, sit reading by the window in the wingback chair, nap when he needed to, and spend much of his time alone with his thoughts. It would be another entirely, come September, to head off early in the morning, walk almost a mile to school, socialize with "friends" who had quietly faded from his life since illness struck, troop from class to class all day long with an armload of texts, meet new teachers, and be barraged with a bewildering flood of new information. And then, at the end of the day, make the long trek back and be ready to face an hour or two of homework in the evening. The mere thought of it filled him with dread.

As he set off to summer school that first morning, he felt like a little kid heading off for his first day of kindergarten. He kept looking back at the house with vague desperation as it faded in the distance. After his last disastrous experience, he wasn't even sure he'd be able to *find* the school. He'd pored over the city street map the night before, and made a rough sketch on a scrap of paper of the route he was to take. He kept it clutched in his hand now while he walked. He still had a knack of tucking things away, never to find them again.

He told himself he wouldn't really need the map, but by the time he'd taken a couple of turns, he found himself in suddenly alien surroundings. He was standing on a corner, staring up at the street signs and checking his map—on which neither of the street names seemed to appear—when someone stole up behind him.

"You took a wrong turn two blocks back, Simon."

"Abbey. What are *you* doing here?"

"I've been shadowing you since you left home. I was

the one who found you the last time you tried to get to school, remember? I was worried you might get lost again, so I decided to follow you."

"Thanks, Abbey. You're a life saver."

"What's that you've got there?"

"Oh, nothing," he said, pushing the piece of paper into his pocket—where it would doubtless vanish forever. He followed meekly after her as she retraced his route. Two blocks back, they came to the street he'd turned off last. She crossed it and headed in exactly the opposite direction.

"You've got a whole different Caledon in your head, Simon. Everything's all switched around, and none of the streets get you where you want to go."

They hadn't gone far before he recognized where they were. He'd wasted valuable time by taking the wrong turn. They had to hurry if he was to make it to school on time. He was fine as long as he was sauntering along at the slow shuffle he'd adopted since he became sick. But two blocks of jogging at a brisk pace now and he was totally depleted. They stopped to rest in the park where Abbey had found him before.

"You sure you're up to this, Simon?"

"Yeah, I'll be fine."

They were a block away when the bell rang. Abbey walked him the rest of the way, wished him luck, and left him at the door.

They'd changed the school since he was last there. The halls were twice as long, the stairs so steep he had to grip the handrail and haul himself up. Someone had jumbled up all the numbers on the classroom doors, and he couldn't find the class he was looking for. He had to poke his head into every room along the hall until he finally found the one where math was being taught. He slipped in the rear door and slid into the nearest seat.

There were a dozen kids in the class, all of them clustered near the front. He recognized a few faces. They seemed to belong to another lifetime.

The teacher was writing on the board. Someone he'd never seen before. She turned around, saw him sitting back there, and motioned him to move up to the front. She asked his name, checked it off her list, and handed him a text from the pile on the corner of her desk. She had that earnest look novice teachers have, like a new car off the lot, before it gets all rusty and worn down.

Her name was Ms. Hart. She'd written it in big block letters on the board. It was the only thing she'd written on the board that he understood. The rest was numbers. He was not good with numbers. They were reviewing decimals. In no time at all he was totally lost.

Abbey was waiting for him in the yard when he came out. She took one look at him and said, "Oh, my god." The walk home was a blank. He felt as if someone had stood him against a wall and shot decimals at him all morning. That night, he went to bed at the same time as Babs. *She* read the bedtime story.

The next day was a bit better. He made it all the way to school with Abbey without stopping. He understood a little more of what was written on the board. Ms. Hart was slow and patient with the class and explained things in a way that almost made sense. He napped in the afternoon, but was nowhere near as exhausted as he'd been the first day.

By the second week, he'd sorted out the route well enough that Abbey decided he could make it on his own. She dropped by in the afternoons after his nap to help him with the homework. With her help, he did well enough on the final exam at the end of the month that Ms. Hart gave him a passing grade.

The last two weeks of August, Abbey went away to a cottage with her family. He hadn't realized just how important she'd become to him, until suddenly she wasn't there. At the start of the second week, a picture postcard came in the mail—a shot of half a dozen cottages huddled on a little slip of a beach backed by rocky cliffs and giant pines.

> *Yup—every bit as exciting as it looks,* she wrote. *Hope you're doing well, Simon. Feels like we've been gone about a hundred years. Max sends Babs a big kiss.*
>> *See you soon.*
>> *Abbey*

He tucked it in the frame of his mirror beside an old photo he'd found that afternoon. He'd been alone in the house. With summer school over and Abbey out of town, time weighed heavily on his hands. He went downstairs to grab a bite to eat, and happened to wander over to the piano. The stack of old sheet music Alice Loudon had given to Mom was out on the stand. A musty smell drifted off it. The topmost piece was a tune from a Gershwin show. He stood at the bench tapping out the opening bars. But when he went to turn the page, he jarred the pile, and the whole lot tumbled to the floor.

He was gathering them up when he noticed a photo that must have fallen out of one of them. It was an old sepia-tinted print of a woman seated at a piano. She was lit from the side, so that the light fell on her arms and her hands at the keyboard, and her face in profile above. It looked so remarkably like Alice Loudon that it could have been her twin. He turned it over. The name of a Paris studio had been stamped on the back, along with a date. It was eighty years old.

At the end of August, a heat wave settled over Caledon like some great bird brooding over its clutch. The upstairs of the house was like an oven. Night after night, Simon lay in the steamy dark listening to the muted strains of Alice Loudon's playing drifting in through the open window.

There was magic in the music. It was full of such sweet sadness, such heartfelt yearning that it nearly moved him to tears. He felt it must have sprung from some deep longing for lost things in *her* life. Yet at the same time it touched his own. He hung on every note. It was as if his sinews had been stretched taut like strings, his bones laid out like keys—and she played upon him.

A door opened onto another world, hidden at the heart of things, beyond the reach and ruin of time. What was lost was found again; what was broken made whole again; what was ill was well again while she played. Memories floated like lilies on the surface of the music. He felt the weight of the tray in his hand as he took Mr. Hawkins his dinner, the hush of the old house as he went about his missions on the second floor, the eager gaze of the mirrors as he moved among them, the book-scented heat of the sunroom as he struggled with the stubborn window, the icy stare of the dog as it peered up at him from the yard.

Eventually, he drifted off. His dreams were full of music, primitive and pulsing, like a heart that had beat steadily since time began. A masked figure came whirling from the shadows of the steamy room, whirling and stomping in time to the urgent rhythm that ran through the scene. As it whirled, he glimpsed its great round eyes, its yawning mouth, its flashing mane. He lay suspended between sleep and consciousness while the music throbbed within him and without.

28

As summer neared its end an uneasy quiet came upon the street. The clamor that had marked the Loudons' first months as they searched the house for the mirror had stopped. The rowdy din of the gang at the end of the street was gone. And now with the singing of the birds eerily absent as well, it felt like the ominous stillness before a storm.

Late in the day, as the sun sank and the shadows lengthened, Alice Loudon would often sit on the porch swing, Caesar by her side. Even from a distance, she did not look well. Her face was gaunt, and there was a noticeable frailty to her. At the height of the summer she'd often sat, in the cool of the evening, swaying lightly back and forth on the swing. But now she sat dead still, a shawl about her shoulders and a blanket over her knees, smoking cigarettes and staring off into an inner distance.

She had spoken of a chronic illness, but Simon had seen no evidence of it till now. She seemed much older than she had mere months before. Despite his dread of her, he could not help but be moved by her struggle with whatever it was that had its hooks in her. He knew what *sick* was, knew it better than he ever imagined he would, and Alice Loudon was *sick*.

The dog never stirred from her side. It sat rigid and alert, its ears twitching at the slightest sound, its eyes ceaselessly panning the street. Now and then it would swing its head around to peer up into her face, but she took no notice as she sat there ghostly and still.

When he was at his sickest, the last thing in the world he worried about was how he looked. But the sicker she became, the more trouble she seemed to take with how she appeared. She had always worn a lot of makeup. He'd noticed it the first time they met—the elaborate eye paint, the bright lipstick, the heavy layer of powder. But now against her gaunt face it seemed garish and sad. What was it that ailed her? he wondered.

He was sitting at the window one evening, reading the "Soul Catchers" manuscript. He eked it out in snippets now as he neared the end. While he remained immersed in the book, it was as if time had stopped, and Mr. Hawkins was with him still. Once he was finished, it would start up again, and there would be no stopping it.

Alice Loudon sat lost in thought on the porch swing, not even bothering to nod as Mrs. Glover walked by with Koko, her poodle. Koko used to bark up a storm when it passed the Loudon's little dog. It didn't bark now. It was clearly afraid of Caesar—as were all the other dogs on the street. Remaining perfectly still by its mistress's side, Caesar followed it with his formidable eyes as it skulked by.

As Mrs. Glover vanished into her house, Simon turned back to the book. A block of added text had been scrawled in the margin of the page in Mr. Hawkins' trembly handwriting. He found the writing too torturous to read in the dim light. As he rose to switch on the light he glanced across the street.

Alice Loudon had vanished.

Moments before, she'd been sitting there as still as a statue. But somehow, in the brief seconds he'd turned his attention back to the book, she'd disappeared.

There hadn't been time enough for her to have gotten up and gone back into the house. And Caesar would certainly have followed her if she had. But the dog was still there, standing by the empty swing as it creaked slowly to rest, and apparently as surprised as Simon at her sudden disappearance.

It sniffed at the blanket lying in a heap on the porch floor, nudging it with its snout as if she might be hidden among the folds. It circled the slack heap several times, then suddenly turned and started across the porch, sniffing at the ground.

As it scooted down the stairs its shadow slid along before it. Following the scent as far as the garden gate, it nosed fretfully at the gap beneath. Then it stepped back and, leaping high into the air, sailed over the fence. On the far side it picked up the scent again and followed it down the side of the house, while its lean shadow slid silently before it along the walk.

It was the day Abbey was supposed to get back from the cottage, and Simon was bursting with news to tell her.

He had just finished reading Babs her bedtime story and switching off her light. Downstairs, Mom was playing the piano. She was supposed to be practicing one of the pieces from the sheet music Alice Loudon had given her. But what he heard drifting up the stairs sounded eerily like the tune Alice Loudon had been whistling in the lane.

He stood at the dresser mirror staring at the old photo that had fallen out of the sheet music. The longer he looked at it, the more convinced he became that it was Alice Loudon sitting there at the keyboard—impossible as it was.

The phone rang. "Telephone for you, Simon," Mom called up the stairs.

"I've got it," he called as he flopped across his bed and picked up the receiver.

"Hey, am I glad to hear from you," he said.

There was a pause on the other end. "I'm happy to hear that," said an older woman's voice.

"I'm sorry. I thought it was someone else."

"I understand. Well, it's Joan Cameron calling, Simon. I hope you remember me."

"Of course," he said, sitting bolt upright on the bed.

"I found your number in the book. The last time I saw you, you weren't well. I hope you're feeling better."

"Yes, much better, thank you." His mind raced as he tried to figure out why she'd be calling him.

"I'm glad to hear that. When we met at the memorial we

were talking about one of our friend Hawkins' mirrors—the one that's gone missing."

"Yes, I remember," he said. He could hear the muffled sound of a TV on the line, then a voice that sounded like Dad's.

"Mom, are you there?" he said into the receiver. There was a soft click on the line.

"Something rather important has come up," said Cameron. "Something that may involve that mirror, and you're the only one I can think to ask about it. I'm afraid we can't really do this over the phone. There's a photo I'd like you to see. I wonder if we might possibly arrange to meet at the museum." Her voice was measured and cool, but an undercurrent of disquiet ran below the calm.

"Of course," he said, his hand trembling as he gripped the phone.

"Would you possibly be free this weekend? Saturday afternoon, say, around two? We could make it some other time if that doesn't work for you."

"No, Saturday should be fine." But all the while, his mind was spinning. The museum was way on the other side of town. Getting there by himself could be a challenge. "Would it be all right if I brought someone with me?" he asked.

"I suppose so," said Cameron. "Is it someone you trust?"

"It is." He would ask Abbey to come—just in case he got lost again.

"Very well, then. Two o'clock it is—at the Egyptian Gallery, in the mummy room. Do you know where that is?"

"Yes, I do."

"Fine. I look forward to seeing you then." And she hung up.

Minutes later, the phone rang again. He picked it up at once. This time it *was* Abbey.

"Whoa, Simon," she said. "You *never* answer the phone."

Someone picked up the downstairs phone. "It's for me," he said, and waited.

"Sorry," said his mom and hung up.

"What's going on, Simon?" asked Abbey.

"I'm not sure," he said. "When did you get back?"

"About an hour ago. It's complete chaos around here, but I wanted to give you a quick call. How are things?"

"A little crazy. I was just talking to Mr. Hawkins' friend, Joan Cameron. How would you like to go to the museum with me this Saturday?"

"The museum? I'll have to check, but I think it'll be all right. And *then* you're going to tell me what's going on, right?"

"Right."

"But not now."

"No, not now."

"You're being *very* mysterious, Simon." In the background he could hear someone call her. "Gotta go," she said. "I'll talk to you later."

"Abbey?'

"Yeah?"

"I'm glad you're back."

"Me too—I think."

29

He lay in bed, unable to sleep. The conversation with Cameron kept circling round in his head. What was it she wanted to ask him about the mirror? She'd made it sound important. He wondered if it might have anything to do with the theft at the museum he'd read about in the paper.

He knew he'd clipped the article and tucked it away somewhere. He slipped quietly out of bed and began looking for it now. He finally found the crumpled thing at the back of his sock drawer. As he read it through again by the light of the bedside lamp his eyes kept drifting to the photo of Cameron that accompanied it. She looked like someone he could trust. He wondered if he dared risk bringing the mirror with him when he went.

He switched off the light and padded to the window. A light rain was falling, and a misty glow encircled the street-lamps. The lights were off in the Loudon house. The world wrapped in sleep. On a night like this, what could possibly be wrong? Yet a current of unease ran below the calm, as it had in Cameron's voice on the phone. He had the sense of darkness stirring, of hidden forces quietly marshaling their powers. And the Egyptian mirror lay at the heart of it all.

He went over to the bed and reached under the mattress. He slid the mirror out and laid it on the bed. It seemed too small a thing to have caused such grief. He would be glad to have it gone, if only for a while.

He ran his fingers over the eye, the undulating pattern that ran around the edge. It was too dark to see much by the faint light through the window, but something felt different about the mirror.

All summer long, he'd withstood the temptation to look in it, for fear it might somehow lead Alice Loudon to him. But now, lulled by the misty calm of the night, and knowing it would soon be out of his hands, perhaps forever, he couldn't resist one last look.

Sitting cross-legged on the bed with the mirror on his lap, he switched on the bedside lamp and looked down. He was shocked by what he saw. The mirror had changed. The surface of it was flecked with green splotches like the scum that forms on standing pools, so that his reflection seemed stricken as well as it stared back at him.

Even as he looked, the image began to ripple lightly, as if the surface had been ruffled by some disturbance beneath. Shadows whirled around the rim. Without warning, he was suddenly swept up in the vortex. The room around him vanished, and he was spun down into the dark.

As his vision cleared, he found himself looking into a room he knew, though he had never viewed it from this angle before. For it was as though he were looking out at the upstairs bedroom in the Hawkins house from the vanity mirror in the corner by the window. Ranged before him on the dressing table were a variety of jars and pots of cosmetics, ivory sticks and spoons, and a hand mirror with a matching brush. Off to one side, there were two wigs on wooden forms—one dark, one fair.

The door in the wall opposite opened, and a figure stood framed in the light. It was utterly dark and devoid of features, like a shadow that had reared itself up from the ground. It wavered there a moment, like a flame worried by a breeze, and then with a weird drifting motion advanced into the room. As it approached the mirror it took on definition. He could make out features now, vague and indistinct, as the figure hovered on the verge of visibility.

It sat down at the table in front of him, so close he could have reached out and touched it, and he realized with a shock it was Alice Loudon. He drew back as she peered into the mirror but then realized, as she studied herself calmly in the glass, that he could not be seen.

She ran her long, thin fingers through the sparse wisps of hair on her head, then slowly over the skin of her face, down across her chin and along her neck as if testing for soundness, pausing here and there to give a light, tentative push. Once, as she prodded, her finger pierced the skin of her cheek as if it were tissue paper, and he caught a shocking glimpse of void through it.

With a look of weary disgust, she dipped her fingers into one of the small jars on the table and smoothed cream over the tear, then over her face and neck. The coating of cream turned the skin satin and lent it substance. The tear on her cheek became a thin red scar, scarcely visible.

She dipped into a little pot and with a practiced finger smoothed rouge on her cheeks and gently worked it in till the skin shone with the flush of life. With the tip of her finger she touched color to each wan lip, then strengthened the line with a brush till they were lush and full.

Next, she turned her attention to her eyes. She mixed a bright green powder from one of the containers with a little saliva on a small wooden spoon, and with the tip of her finger stroked an emerald sheen on the lid of each eye. Wetting the end of one of the pointed ivory sticks with her mouth, she dipped it in a small pot of black powder and drew a bold line above the lashes of each eyelid, extending it with a flourish well beyond the corner of the eye. In the same way, she lined the lower lids, and with a small brush darkened the lashes. Finally, she painted in two broad, arching brows above the eyes.

Turning from the mirror, she lifted the dark wig from its form and fit it securely in place on her head. From a small jewelry box she withdrew two curious gold earrings shaped like flies. With a slight tilt of her head she hooked them into her earlobes, then took out a matching necklace and fastened it about her neck. The transformation was complete. She had passed from shadow into form. She sat back and studied herself in the glass with wide, searching eyes. Turning her head this way and that, she softened a line here, strengthened one there, framed her hair about her face with the brush.

Then, as she leaned in close to the glass to touch up the corner of one eye, she suddenly froze. Turning toward the window, she started to rise from her seat, then abruptly wheeled back—and brought her face up flush against the glass.

Simon sprang back in shock on the bed, and something brushed him lightly on the arm. He spun around, and there stood Babs by the bed, thumb tucked in her mouth. She had clearly gone over the rail again, breaking her fall on the cushions below.

"Dimon, I wan dink," she said as she scrambled up onto the bed beside him and leaned down to look in the mirror. He quickly pulled his pillow over it and tumbled them both out of bed.

"Okay, Babs, let's get you a drink," he said shakily.

She sat on the lid of the toilet while he ran the water in the sink till it was cold and filled her cup. He smoothed her hair mechanically with his hand as she drank. He felt totally spooked, half of him still in the mirror world, half in this one. As he rinsed the cup he caught sight of a dark shape looming behind him in the mirror. He let out a startled cry, and then realized it was just Dad's dressing gown hanging on the door hook.

Babs looked at him with wide eyes. She took him by the hand and they padded down the hall to her room. Her sheets were in a tangle. He smoothed them out, tucked her in, and patted her back for a few minutes. But when he turned to go, she begged him not to leave.

He lay down on the cushions by the crib and held her hand through the bars until it grew slack in his own and her breathing came slow and deep. He would gladly have stayed there with her all night, but with nothing to cover himself with, it was cold on the floor, and every time he closed his eyes he was back in the mirror world again. Finally, he got up and tiptoed back to his room.

He lifted the pillow off the mirror and, summoning all his courage, looked down into it. But the vision had vanished, and it was just his own frightened face that looked back. He wished he'd never touched the mirror, but it was too late for wishing. He tucked it back under the mattress. His one hope was that what he'd seen had not been real, that Alice Loudon hadn't actually seen him in the mirror.

He stole to the window and lifted the edge of the curtain. The old house sat dark and still. There were no lights on in the front bedroom, no hint that anything out of the ordinary had occurred. He drew a deep breath. He'd been foolish to work himself into such a state. The vision had no more substance than a dream. But he'd been reckless to look in the mirror, all the same. He would take it with him when he went to see Cameron—and good riddance if he never set eyes on it again.

As he turned from the window he heard a sound. It was a sound he knew well, and it sent a shiver through him. He looked back at the Loudon's porch. The swing was cloaked in shadows, but he could clearly hear its faint rhythmic creak as it swung to and fro.

Si-mon, Si-mon, it seemed to say in its creaky voice.

Suddenly a match flared in the dark, illumining Alice Loudon's face as she lit a cigarette. The same strange earrings he'd seen in the vision dangled from her ears. The same necklace hung about her neck. As she leaned in close to the flame and blew it out, he could have sworn she cast a quick glance his way.

PART III
THE MUMMY ROOM

By providing a home for the double in the tomb, the mirror
prevented it from wandering off into the world
and causing mischief among the living.

-Randall Hawkins, *Soul Catchers*

30

Bright and early Saturday morning, Mom and Dad headed off with Babs to spend the day at the beach. It was
a Labor Day weekend tradition: a day in the sun, wedged
blanket to blanket on the hot sand with all the other
families who had the same idea—like a catch of cod laid
out on a dock to dry. They looked forward to it all summer
long. It would be well after dark before they were back.

Simon had convinced them he wasn't feeling well
enough to go. The jolting and jarring of the hot car made
him sick to his stomach at the best of times. Dad didn't
need much convincing. Last summer, locked in traffic on
the steamy highway on the way home, Simon had rolled
down the window and spewed down the side of the car.

It was just a day trip, but Mom packed like they were
heading off for a week. As Simon ushered Babs out to the
waiting car that morning, he heard Dad muttering under
his breath as he fought to fit the stroller into the crowded
trunk. Mom sat quietly in the front seat with the picnic
basket on her lap. As Simon buckled Babs into the car

seat, pail and shovel by her side, Mom looked up in the rear view mirror at him.

"You be good, Simon," she said. "We shouldn't be late."

No sooner were they out of sight than he set to work. After the incident with the mirror earlier that week there was no way he was going to simply walk out the door with it undisguised. He thought about tucking it down the back of his pants and wearing a jacket over it. But it was too hot to be wearing a jacket, and even with it on, the edge of the mirror showed below, and it looked like he had a dinner plate shoved down his pants. Besides, he couldn't stand to have it up against him now. It felt somehow alive.

He considered putting it in a bag, but every bag he tried felt transparent. He was convinced Alice Loudon would see straight through it and know instantly what he was up to. Then he remembered the old canvas rucksack he'd had with him the night they found the mirror. He fetched it from the garage and slid the mirror into it. And suddenly it felt safe. All the same, when he went to meet Abbey in the park at noon, he left by the back door and stole away along the lane.

As they hurried off along the winding streets, he cast an occasional look back to see if they were being followed, but it seemed they'd managed to slip off without arousing suspicion.

Soon, the walk began to take its toll. The museum was on the far side of town. For a healthy Simon it would have been a brisk forty-five minute walk. But for sick Simon it was a different story entirely. He was totally wrung out before they were halfway there.

By then they'd left the shady side streets behind and were walking along a sweltering midtown street in the midst of a crowd of Saturday shoppers. Abbey steered him over to a bench by a bus stop and sat him down. She went to check the schedule posted on the pole. A crosstown bus that would take them steps from the museum was due by soon. She sat down beside him while they waited for it to come.

A guy with a guitar was busking on the corner across the street. He had his guitar case open in front of him and a black and white terrier with a red bandana around its neck on a blanket beside him. Abbey kept looking over at him.

The bus came at last. They headed straight for the back, where they could be alone. As the bus drove off, Abbey stood staring out the rear window at the corner where the busker was playing.

"What is it?" he asked.

"For a moment I could have sworn I saw Alice Loudon's dog sitting there beside that guy, looking over at us. But it's just some little dog with a bandana around its neck." She sat down and shook her head. "Just seeing things," she said.

Since the incident with the mirror, Simon had been doing nothing *but*. In every reflective surface he encountered, he saw Alice Loudon looking back at him as she had that night. He had to cover the mirror in his room again so he could sleep.

"So what was that with your mom the other night?" said Abbey.

"I think she was listening in on my call with Joan Cameron," he said. "And then when you called right after, she picked up again."

"But she always answers the phone, Simon. And you *never* do."

"Maybe, but since she started those piano lessons with Alice Loudon, she's different somehow. And she's not the only one. The kids look like zombies when they shuffle back and forth to lessons. A few days back, one of them stepped off the curb right into the path of a car. He just missed being hit, but there was no reaction at all. I'm telling you, Abbey, there's something strange going on. It's like the life has been drained from them."

"What did Joan Cameron have to say?"

"She thinks I might be able to help her with something about the mirror," he said. "She wants to show me a photo she found."

"She doesn't know you have it, then?"

"No, but I decided to bring it along," he said, tapping the knapsack. "To tell you the truth, I'll be glad to be rid of it for a while."

He told her about his experience with the mirror: the shadowy form he'd seen standing in the doorway of the Hawkins' bedroom; its slow, terrifying transformation into Alice Loudon as he watched through the mirror; her sudden awareness that he was there.

"Geez, Simon, that's about the scariest thing I've ever heard," she said.

The bus passed under a bridge. As the outer world went dark his reflection loomed up in the bus window beside him, with Abbey's next to him. But now, from the far end of the reflected seat, another passenger peered back. As he spun around to look, the bus plunged back into day. The seat stood empty in the light.

"Everything all right, Simon?"

"Yeah." He began rummaging through his pockets. "I found an old photo while you were away. A picture of a woman playing a piano. It fell out of the sheet music Alice Loudon loaned my mom. It looks exactly like her."

"Probably is," she said. "It's her music, after all."

He found the photo and handed it to her. She took a long look.

"That's her, all right."

"Check out the date on the back of it," he said.

She flipped it over and looked. "That's not possible, Simon. It's over eighty years old." She turned it and studied the photo again.

Simon looked up and saw the museum go by. He reached up and yanked the bell cord. The driver swung into the curb and came to a jarring halt at the stop. He glared up in the rearview mirror at them as they hurried out the rear door.

31

It seemed like all the families in town that hadn't gone to the beach had wound up at the museum. As Abbey and Simon came through the doors into the foyer they found themselves in the midst of a noisy crowd lining up to get in.

The museum was a monument to an age of grandeur that defied the busy rush of time. It looked down with a cool, granite gaze on the mob milling about its figured marble floor. High above the bustle, dust motes drifted lazily in the tinted light of the stained glass windows set in the wall of the foyer, and the ghosts of time past leaned over the rails of the upper galleries and looked silently down. Here time had stopped, as surely as the large block of magnetite in the Mineral Room would stop the watches of unwary visitors who ventured too near.

Abbey craned her neck to peer up at the vaulted ceiling as Simon paid the harried young cashier. Rather than wait for an elevator, they started up the shallow marble stairs. Flight by flight they climbed, slowly circling the echoing stairwell that pierced the building from top to bottom like the hub round which it turned. Pausing on a landing between floors to catch their breath, Abbey took a long look down.

"You sure you know where we're going, Simon?" They had already passed three floors without pausing, and were now the only ones left on the stairs.

"I'm sure," he said, peering up the well. "We're nearly there."

It felt as though the higher they climbed, the farther back in time they went. So that when they stood finally at the top, facing the arched entrance to the Egyptian Gallery, the day-to-day world had faded to a dull murmur far below, and they had been spirited back to ancient times.

A hush fell over them as they slipped past the solemn stone figures flanking the entrance. Although it was a busy day at the museum, there were only a handful of visitors here. Most families were drawn to the glitzier galleries on the lower floors with their towering dinosaurs and their interactive displays. Few families ventured as far as the upper floor, except to see the mummy. Here things had remained unchanged for years.

The gallery was a set of three high-ceilinged rooms. The outer walls of the first two were pierced by tall lancet windows that cast spears of sunlight on the wooden floor. The third, and smallest, was the mummy room. It was windowless, cast in constant shadow to safeguard its delicate contents.

Three display cases ran lengthwise down the center of the first two rooms, with four more down each side, set sidewise in the space between pillar and wall. As Abbey and Simon drifted by, their reflections slid on the surface of the cases alongside them.

It was one of those places where everything that had ever happened seemed somehow present still, preserved in silence like the ancient artifacts in their cases: vessels of stone and clay, statues of wood with inlaid eyes, amuletic jewelry of gold and semi-precious stones, miniature clay figures meant to serve the needs of those with whom they'd been buried in the afterlife. Ranged on their glass shelves in glass cases, they seemed to float on air.

Approaching the mummy room, Simon felt the same unease he'd felt here as a child: the sense that he was seeing something he shouldn't, that he was violating the repose of the dead and would in some way be punished for it. It was all he could do not to turn and flee down the echoing stairs, out into the daylight world again.

Dr. Cameron was nowhere in sight. As he lingered in the doorway waiting, Abbey entered the room and approached the mummy case. She bent low to study the ancient figure asleep behind the glass. Seeing her lent him courage, and he too ventured in. They stood on opposite sides of the case, peering in at the mummy and, past it, at one another.

It lay there in its painted wooden coffin. The lid had been removed, raised up on four thin wires, so that it hung suspended above the mummy and cast its shadow over it. They had to lean close to the case to see clearly— as close as three confidantes conversing in a crowded room. But here it was an intimacy of silence spanning the centuries.

The figure was swaddled tight in its cocoon of fragile cloth. Only the bandaging that covered its face had been removed. The skin was dark and glossy, like polished leather stretched tight over the skull. The lips were drawn back thin and taut from the teeth, the eyelids sunk deep in their sockets. The nose was thin and horny like the beak of a bird; the hair like wisps of cotton wool, the color of ochre. It was a dreadful, drawing thing.

Simon was reminded of the shadowy figure at the vanity in his vision. He had a sudden, almost palpable sense of Alice Loudon's presence.

"I'm just going to walk around a bit," he said and fled the shadowed room and the aura of unease that hung over it.

Sunlight spilled through the gallery windows, glinting off the cases. He kept seeing Alice Loudon looking back at him from the glass. Suddenly, he stopped in his tracks. He slowly approached a tall case tucked behind a pillar near the mummy room. It contained a life-size waxwork figure of a woman in Egyptian costume applying her makeup.

She sat at a table on which various pots and jars of cosmetics were arrayed alongside small brushes and tapered sticks. They looked like those he'd seen on the vanity table in his vision. The mannequin held a mirror in her hand. It was only a model, but mounted on the wall behind were three ancient bronze mirrors, each covered in a dull green coating of corrosion.

A figure came up quietly behind him while he was lost in thought. He saw the dim reflection in the glass of the case and swung around.

"Sorry, Simon. I didn't mean to frighten you," said Dr. Cameron. "I see you've found our mirrors. That one's quite like the Hawkins mirror, isn't it?

Abbey had wandered over from the other room. "I'd like you to meet my friend Abbey," he said. "Abbey, this is Dr. Cameron."

"Please, 'Cameron' will do just fine. It's what everyone here calls me." She extended her hand. "Pleased to meet you, Abbey."

"While we're alone for a moment, I'd like to show you something," she said and led them to a case on the far side of the room.

"The items on display here were discovered in the late nineteenth century by Edmund Walker, during the course of excavating an ancient Egyptian town that had housed a workforce of pyramid builders. He found them hidden in a hollow under the floor of one of the houses."

Several artifacts were arranged on a bed of sun-bleached velvet in the case. There was a pair of ivory clappers carved at the tips into the shape of hands, half a dozen small glazed animal figures, and the tattered remains of a painted canvas mask with a bright red mouth, wide encircled eyes, and a lion's mane.

As he looked at the mask, Simon was suddenly reminded of the whirling figure in his dream.

"These things likely belonged to a magician," said Cameron. "Ancient Egyptians used magic as a means of protection against the many dangers they faced in their world. These clappers would have been used as part of a dance performed by the magician to frighten off demons.

These animal figures represent the forces at the magician's disposal and were animated by means of a spell. And this mask was likely worn by the magician, acting in the role of the god, while performing magical rites."

"As you can see, there's an item missing from the case," said Cameron.

A long, thin silhouette was clearly visible on the velvet cloth.

"It was a bronze snake wand, a potent instrument used against evil forces. It disappeared some months back. Since the case showed no signs of being tampered with, I assumed it had simply been removed by a curator, or sent on loan to another institution and the paperwork had somehow been mislaid. But then, two weeks ago, another item went missing."

She led them to a case over by the entrance to the mummy room.

"The trove of objects from the magician's kit was a remarkable find. But less than a month later, it was overshadowed by the discovery of an undisturbed grave by a team excavating the large cemetery that lay just outside the town.

"This was the cemetery for the workers and their families, and consisted of simple graves dug in the desert sand. Humble graves like this were overlooked by grave robbers, who concentrated on the rich graves of the wealthy that were cut in the rock of the surrounding hills. But in this particular grave, a shaft grave cut down to the bedrock in the sand, a painted wooden coffin containing an astonishingly well-preserved mummy was found, with a very fine necklace about its neck, and several large amulets tucked among the linen wrappings. Those items were displayed in this case. As you can see, the necklace is missing.

"Now, one missing object could easily be an accident, but two is something different. I contacted the police at once and went back through the acquisition records of both to gather as many details as I could about them. And there I stumbled upon an even greater mystery."

She swept her eyes around the room. "This place no longer feels safe to me since these strange disappearances. I suggest we talk in my office."

She walked them back briskly through the gallery and onto the balcony overlooking the busy foyer below. Leading them over to an old elevator with ornamented brass doors, she pushed the button. The sweep hand over the doors jerked in fits and starts from floor to floor until it reached theirs. The doors slid open, and they went in.

The small old elevator creaked and groaned as it carried them down into in the depths of the museum. An eerie silence had settled over them, broken only by the light *ping* of the elevator as it descended past the other floors and lurched to a halt at the lowest level.

32

Cameron led them through a labyrinth of dim hallways and stopped before a door with her name stenciled on the frosted glass. She unlocked it and ushered them into a small, low-ceilinged room. There were books and papers piled everywhere. As she cleared a space for them to sit, Simon ran his eyes around the room.

The tops of the bookcases were lined with ancient figurines. Among them was a statuette of a black dog with pricked ears and a pointed snout. It rested on its belly, its head erect, and its huge eyes staring dead ahead. He stiffened when he saw it. Abbey noticed him staring and looked up too.

Several framed photos hung on the wall behind the desk. He'd seen one of them before: a photo of Hawkins standing with a young woman beside a deep shaft in the desert sand.

"That was taken on the site where Hawkins and I first met," said Cameron. "I was a raw grad student on my first dig. He was a well-respected worker in the field. As a result of something that happened on that dig I developed an interest in ancient Egyptian magic. I've written several books on the subject down the years. This chaos you see around you here is another in the making.

"It was partly due to my interest in Egyptian magic that Hawkins first approached me with the mirror. It was rumored to possess magical powers, and he wanted to know if I'd ever come across anything like it in my studies. I told him that the figure of the goddess Beset worked into the handle spoke to its having served some magical purpose, but it was unlike anything I'd seen. Yet because of its pristine condition, we both agreed the mirror must be a fake.

"But when I was going through the acquisition records of the missing objects, I came upon something very strange that I'd like you to see."

Abbey gave Simon a nudge and nodded toward the rucksack.

"We brought something *you* might like to see," he said and slid the mirror from the bag.

Cameron's eyes widened. "How on earth did you come by this?"

"We dug it up," said Abbey.

"Dug it up?"

"At the memorial, you told me the last time you talked to Mr. Hawkins, he said he'd decided to hide the mirror to keep it safe," said Simon.

"That's right. He'd taken into his head that there were prowlers around the house, and they were after it."

"There *were* odd things going on around the house," said Simon. "I saw something too." And he told Cameron about the strange dog he'd seen in the Hawkins yard. "It looked like that," he said, nodding toward the statue on the shelf.

"That's Anubis, the black jackal-like dog," said Cameron. "Guardian of magical secrets, defender against evil forces. A life-size statue of Anubis guarded the tomb of King Tut. Go on."

"When I saw it a second time, sitting in exactly the same place, I thought it might be a shadow or something, so I snuck into the yard to see. There was no sign a dog had ever been there. But then I heard a growl from the bushes, and I saw eyes peering out through the leaves. Human eyes."

Once the stopper was off, the story streamed out like a genie from a bottle. He told Cameron about the letter Hawkins had received from Winstanley, the dealer he'd bought the mirror from, warning him about a woman with a scar on her cheek who was after the mirror, and a beast that prowled by night. He told her his suspicions that the new people who'd moved into the Hawkins house weren't the relatives they claimed to be.

Abbey told her about the obituary they'd found in one of the Hawkins' old photo albums.

"Before moving in, the new people used to come by the house at night," said Simon. "They went through the place room by room. I think they were looking for the mirror. They threw out all kinds of things a real relative wouldn't have. Like those photo albums and the manuscript of Mr. Hawkins' book."

"We rescued it all," said Abbey.

"You mean you have Hawkins' manuscript?" said Cameron, leaning forward excitedly in her chair.

Abbey nodded. "Then one day Simon noticed a glint in the Hawkins garden."

"I'd read an article by Mr. Hawkins in an old journal, where he said that people once believed the best way to keep something safe was to bury it," Simon added.

"And so you thought he might have hidden the mirror in the garden."

"One night, before the new people moved in, we snuck into the yard and dug in the spot where Simon had seen the glint," said Abbey.

"And we found it," he said.

Cameron put the mirror down and examined it on both sides through a large magnifying glass mounted on the desk. Two large folders lay nearby. She opened one and sifted through some old photos. Removing one, she studied it under the glass.

"Incredible," she muttered as she moved between the photo and the mirror. Swinging the magnifying glass away, she leaned back in her chair. For a long while she was silent. Then she got up and walked over to the photo of Hawkins and her standing by the shaft in the sand.

"I look at the young woman in this photo, and it all seems like a lifetime ago. But then I look down that shaft and time dissolves, and I'm back there again. Something happened on that dig—something that changed me, forever.

"Hawkins had discovered that tomb shaft buried in the sand near a ruined temple. He found several artifacts scattered in the rubble at the bottom, but no sign of a burial chamber. I was lowered down on the end of a rope, and was busy sifting through the rubble by the light of my headlamp to see if there was more to be found, when I dislodged a large stone in the wall of the shaft. It revealed a narrow tunnel that opened for several feet and was then blocked by a wall that had been partially broken through.

"I called up to say what I'd found, but there was no reply. Then, in my excitement and inexperience, I did something I should never have done. I crawled into the tunnel. The sides were slick with damp and the brick was soft, but I was set on reaching the wall to see if it opened onto the missing burial chamber. I inched along on my elbows as far as the wall and was clearing the rubble around the opening to see what lay the other side, when without warning a section of the tunnel collapsed behind me.

"I lay there, pinned in the dark, afraid to stir in case the entire thing came down on my head. Suddenly, the light of my headlamp fell on a pair of eyes peering out at me through the opening in the wall. Rather than alarm me, there was in those eyes such a sense of strength and calm that it helped allay my panic.

"I have no idea how long I lay there before I was aware of voices in the shaft and was pulled free by a rescue party. The tunnel was shored up, and at the end of it, beyond the broken wall, they found a burial chamber, rich with grave goods. Among them was a life-size statue of painted wood and plaster. It was found nowhere near the wall, but as soon as I saw it I knew those eyes."

Cameron walked slowly back to the desk and sat down on the edge of it.

"When that second artifact, the mummy's necklace, recently went missing," she said, "I went down to the archives and pulled the accession files on it and the other missing item. They're very old, as you can see, among the oldest of our records. I was looking for exact details of the missing objects, so that I could provide the police with a full description, and alert the antiquities dealers to be on the lookout for them.

"Even back then it was standard practice to make sketches or take photos of each find on site as soon as possible, so that a detailed record would exist in the event that an object should suffer damage, or go missing. Bronze objects in particular are susceptible to a rapid form of corrosion called bronze disease when suddenly introduced to the atmosphere after having been buried under the ground for so long. And it is not uncommon for an object to go missing. Ancient artifacts can fetch a high price on the illegal market, and theft is a constant problem on any dig.

"That, in fact, is precisely what happened here. One of the artifacts found with the mummy in its coffin that day, along with the necklace and the amulets, vanished from the site and was never seen again. It was likely stolen by one of the workers.

"It was a bronze mirror. All that remained of it was the description of it in this file, and the photo they took that day—this photo." She took the photo she'd been studying under the glass and set it down on the edge of the desk in front of them.

"As soon as I saw it, it reminded me of Hawkins' mirror: the unusual figure forming the handle, the incised eye on the face of it. And laying the two side by side now, I see that even the snaking pattern around the rim is the same.

"The mirror discovered on that dig has all the signs of corrosion one would expect to see in an ancient bronze object. Bronze is an alloy of copper and tin. The elements are unstable and, over time, revert to their original state, forming a solid coating over the object. The process is irreversible. The corrosion doesn't sit on the surface like a stain that can be removed. It *is* the surface.

"When Hawkins showed me the mirror he'd bought in London, it had absolutely no trace of corrosion. It was that more than anything that convinced us it was a forgery. Yet as I compare it now with the photo of the artifact stolen from that dig almost a hundred years ago, it's beyond doubt the same mirror—somehow magically renewed. Though there are signs of decay on it now that weren't there when I first saw it."

"Even in the short time we've had it, it's changed," said Simon. "It's as if it is sick." The words spilled out without thought. And as they did, the image of Alice Loudon sitting wrapped in her shawl on the porch flashed into his mind.

"What is it, Simon?" said Abbey.

"Mr. Hawkins calls mirrors 'soul catchers' in his book. He says that ancient people believed the double they saw in the mirror was their soul, and that they used to bury mirrors with their dead to keep the soul nearby."

"That's true," said Cameron. "The ancient Egyptians commonly buried mirrors with their dead. They believed that the *ka*—what we would call the soul— needed a place to dwell in the tomb. That place was very often a mirror.

The offerings they brought to the tomb were meant to feed the *ka*, so that it wouldn't wander. There's a chilling image in one ancient manuscript of the *Book of the Dead*, depicting the *ka* as a shadowlike figure wandering from the tomb."

Abbey's mouth fell open. She looked at Simon. "Tell her," she said. "It's okay if it sounds crazy."

"Alice Loudon dropped by our house for a visit right after she moved in," he said. "My mom told her about my illness, and Mrs. Loudon said she had a chronic illness herself. She looked older than she had when Abbey and I saw her in the park just a month before. And high up on one cheek, half-hidden by her makeup, she had a scar, like the scar Winstanley talked about in his letter.

"She offered to make some herbal medicine for me. She brought it by the house a couple of days later. I didn't take it, but I saved it. I have it here." He took the packet from his pocket and handed it to Cameron.

"It's the most awful smelling stuff you can imagine," said Abbey.

Cameron opened the packet and examined the powder closely. She took a sniff and flinched a little. "Go on," she said.

"I've never seen her eat or drink," he said. "That day she was at the house, she took the tea and cookie my mother offered but didn't touch either of them. And Abbey's watched her in her yard, taking the food her husband prepares for her and dumping it secretly onto the grass for their dog. It was just a little rust-colored pup when she first moved in, but the bigger it gets the more it reminds me, especially at night, of the dog I saw in Mr. Hawkins' yard.

"I swear she never sleeps. She's up at all hours, playing the piano or sitting on her porch, smoking. One night last week, she was sitting there with the dog, looking really sick. I turned away a moment, and when I looked back she'd *vanished*. Just vanished. The shawl she'd been wearing was lying in a heap on the floor.

"After you called this week, I took the mirror out. I had kept it tucked away, thinking she might be able to sense when I was using it. But I looked in it now, and I saw something in it—a sort of vision. It's happened to me before. Mr. Hawkins said his wife used to see things in the mirror, too.

"I saw Alice Loudon standing in the doorway of the bedroom in the Hawkins house. She was faint, featureless—like a shadow. She drifted into the room and sat down at the vanity. It was like I was on the other side of the mirror, watching her. She put on her makeup. She used pots and brushes and little pointed sticks, like the ones in the display case in the gallery upstairs. As she put on the makeup, she became more *real*. Suddenly, she looked up, and it was like she saw me watching her."

A faint, high laughter echoed in the hall outside the room. Cameron put a finger to her lips and stole over to the door. She listened a moment, and then, with a swift motion, threw it open.

33

They heard a scurrying sound somewhere off in the labyrinth of passageways.

"Wait here," said Cameron and set off down the hall to investigate.

Abbey drew Simon back into the room and locked the door behind them. She glanced up at the cold eyes of Anubis glaring down on them from the bookcase. Simon felt the weight of the old building pressing down upon them. The minutes crept by.

Finally, there was a sound of hurried footsteps in the hall, and a ghostly figure rapped on the frosted glass.

"It's me," said Cameron, and Abbey opened the door.

"Whoever it was got away," said Cameron as she slipped back into the room. "The elevator doors closed just before I got there; a couple of kids running in the halls, no doubt. It often happens on holidays."

She pretended to be calm, but the incident had clearly unnerved them all. When they spoke now, it was in hushed tones—as though the ground they stood on had shifted, and they were in a different, more dangerous place than they'd been before.

Cameron took up the mirror and turned it in her hand.

"When I asked you to come today," she said, "it was to show you a photo of a mirror I'd stumbled on in an old file, to see if it looked to you as much like Hawkins' mirror as it did to me. I had no idea you had your own story to tell. Yet I wonder, now, if it might not all be part of one story—a story steeped in ancient magic.

"Here we have a mirror that went missing from an excavation site late in the nineteenth century, only to turn up a century later in the hands of a dealer who purchased it at auction, and then sold it on to our friend Hawkins in order to be rid of it. A mirror so untouched by time that both Hawkins and I wrote it off as a fake. Yet the woman who pursued it when Winstanley had it, and then Hawkins after him, is pursuing it still.

"Who is this mysterious Alice Loudon, and why is she so desperate to obtain this mirror? Clearly, she is deeply versed in Egyptian lore. This herbal potion is the type of remedy an Egyptian magician might have prepared. What you smell is dung, a common ingredient in ancient remedies, mixed here with a variety of medicinal herbs. The cosmetics and their application are something only someone versed in the ways of ancient Egypt would know. And then there's that dog of hers, an ancient breed dating back to the Egyptian pharaohs and associated with Anubis, the Egyptian god of magic.

"She has some mysterious illness, she says, and seems to be rapidly failing. And at the same time, the mirror is decaying—as if the two were somehow connected. But how?" Circling the desk, she stopped in front of the photo of herself and Hawkins standing by the tomb shaft. She stared at it fixedly, as if the answer might lie there.

"That was my first dig—and my last," she said. "Hawkins' way and mine diverged after that. His to further explorations, mine to the study of ancient magic, and the task of tending the things that we, and others like us, had wrested from the dark.

"But it changed me, changed the way I thought of the past. The illusion of distance dissolved. It seemed to me that the artifacts we unearthed were like windows in time, and there were moments when past and present stood on either side of that window and caught a glimpse of one another—as I had that day.

"Was it an experience of magic I had down in that tunnel? I don't know. But to this day I see those eyes peering out through the hole in the wall at me, like the eye engraved on the face of this mirror."

Simon and Abbey sat spellbound in their seats.

"I said this was a story steeped in ancient magic," she went on. "Consider these recent thefts at the museum. The first was from a case that housed a collection of objects belonging to an ancient magician. The second, from a case that contained the grave goods discovered with a remarkably well-preserved mummy on the same dig. Why were those two cases targeted? Why were those two objects taken, when many more valuable artifacts were left untouched? Could there be a connection between them?

"The necklace had been buried with the mummy in her coffin. So too, as it turns out, had this mirror—a mirror with a most unusual handle in the shape of the goddess Beset. Now, Beset was a goddess beloved by the common people of ancient Egypt. She was invoked in many magical rituals around the protection of women and children. One of the objects in the case from which the snake wand was stolen is a Beset mask, worn by the magician while acting in the role of the goddess during such rituals.

"At that time most magicians in Egypt were men. The only comparable collection of magical objects that has been found belonged to a temple priest. But the discovery of these objects under the floor of a common dwelling in a pyramid workers' town is compelling evidence that there also existed at that time a class of communal magicians who tended to the needs of ordinary people in their daily lives.

"In the pyramid workers' town, the men spent much of their time away at the pyramid site, so the day-to-day running of the town fell largely to the women. I've long believed these things belonged to a female magician. They would have been used in the rituals she was called upon to perform: casting protective spells against disease, and physical dangers such as snakebites, scorpion stings, and against the constant threat of wild animals. But especially against the dangerous forces that threatened young children, and women in childbirth.

"Is it possible that the mummy who was buried with this mirror might in fact be the magician who wore that mask? Was it perhaps by force of magic that she was so well preserved?"

Simon had listened with rapt attention to every word she spoke, thinking and wondering all the while.

"Then the mirror would have been home to the magician's double in the tomb, wouldn't it?" he said.

"Yes, that's right," said Cameron.

"Then what happened to it when the mirror was stolen?" asked Abbey.

Simon stared down at the mirror. He thought of Babs and her mirror friend, and again of his own double, who'd slipped from the mirror when he was sick and wandered free. He remembered the vision in the mirror of the man running through the desert in the night, and the figure flowing out of the mirror he carried. He looked at Cameron, who looked back and slowly nodded. And he summoned the courage to say what till then he'd only dared to think.

"It escaped from the mirror," he said and sat silent as the weight of it settled upon them. "And maybe when it did, the mirror returned to the way it had appeared in ancient times, when the double first went into it."

"Then you're saying that Alice Loudon is—what? The magician's double?" said Abbey.

"Yes," he said.

"But if she somehow managed to get free of the mirror, why would she be seeking it so desperately now?"

"When the double was tied to the tomb, it took the form of a shadow," said Cameron. "Perhaps when it was loosed into the world, it became a creature of flesh and blood. But because it was immortal—"

"It didn't need to eat or drink," said Simon, suddenly understanding.

"And it wouldn't have aged," said Abbey. "That would explain that photo you found, Simon, where she looked exactly the same eighty years ago."

He took the photo from his pocket and handed it to Cameron. She studied it intently and set it down on the desk.

"But then, for some reason, things began to change," she said. "*She* began to change, to age. And perhaps she realized she was linked to the mirror after all—that her life depended upon it somehow. So she began to seek it out. When Hawkins came into possession of it, he became the object of her pursuit, as the dealer Winstanley had before. And as you have now that it's come into your hands.

"There's something I'd like you to see." She turned in her chair and switched on a small monitor sitting on one of the bookshelves behind her. "Another mystery surrounding the recent thefts. All this talk of shadows made me think of it."

An image flickered onto the screen.

"This is the footage from a security camera in the gallery at the time of the most recent theft," she said. "I won't tell you how many times I've watched it, searching for some clue as to how that necklace could possibly have disappeared."

People came and went, drifting briefly onto the screen, drifting away. For long periods the gallery stood empty. She fast-forwarded the tape; the time highlighted on the image sped by. Suddenly she stopped.

"Now look closely," she said. "There, in the background, a figure appears at the entrance to the room. Do you see?"

They saw a blurry figure pause briefly in the doorway without entering the room and then walk on by, beyond the range of the camera.

"Now watch," said Cameron. She sped up the tape again. Minutes flew by on the monitor. The same figure paused and passed by several times. She returned the tape to normal speed as the figure appeared again in the doorway. But now as it passed, a shadow suddenly appeared on the floor near the entrance to the room.

"Do you see that?" said Cameron.

"Yes," said Simon. As he watched the shadow drift slowly across the floor he pictured the shadow slipping down the porch stairs and along the side of the house with Caesar in pursuit. The shadow on the monitor fell briefly over the display case and moved on.

"When I first saw it, I couldn't make any sense of it," said Cameron. "I thought it must be the shadow of a passing cloud or plane outside. Now, I'm not so sure."

Abbey had her nose pressed close to the screen. "Wait," she said. "Did you see that glint on the glass of the case? Can you go back and pause it there?"

Cameron slowly rewound the tape.

"There. Right *there*," said Abbey. "Can you zoom in on that?"

Cameron zoomed in on the image fixed on the screen. It was blurry, and it distorted as it draped over the edge of the case. But there, reflected in the glass, was a face. The face of Alice Loudon.

They stood dumbfounded, staring at the frozen image, till Cameron reached out and switched off the monitor.

She walked back to her desk and sat down. For a long while, she looked down at the mirror, lost in thought.

"Supposing Alice Loudon is who we imagine her to be," she said at last. "Why would she want these things that have gone missing?"

"To make magic with," said Simon.

"In order to get hold of the mirror," added Abbey.

"I may be mad, but I think you're right," said Cameron. "What she intends to do with it, I don't know. But I fear her power, with it in her possession. Now, I'm no magician, but I've studied Egyptian magic for many years, and there's one thing I know for certain—the only way to meet magic is *with* magic.

"Normally, we'd be no match for her. But she is in a weakened state, and she's not expecting to be opposed— certainly not by magic. Now, Egyptian magic is a very complex art. It depends on combining exactly the right words, with the right actions and the right materials, at the right time. If any of these is lacking, the spell will not work.

"The first thing I need to do is go back over the ancient texts to see if I can find a spell to suit our purposes, or else craft a new one. It will take me a little time, but it's important that we move cautiously, for I expect we'll have just one chance. I'll call you when I'm done, and we can plan our next move.

"In the meantime, I'll keep the mirror here with me. I want you both to be very careful. I'm not convinced Alice Loudon is evil, but she is certainly desperate—and dangerous because of that. She seems to be biding her time at the moment. But if anything happens, anything at all, you can reach me at this number." She gave them her card. "You should probably be going. The building will be closing soon. I'll walk you to the elevator."

They wound their way through the maze of flickering passageways. Cameron called the elevator down and Simon and Abbey stepped in. They left her standing alone in the dim hallway as the doors closed and they ascended to the upper world.

The visit had totally drained Simon. He was so tired it was all he could do to put one foot in front of the other. Abbey insisted on walking him safely home. They came in by the back way, along the lane, to avoid being seen.

The lane was lined with old garages separated by high wooden fences. Some were still being used for cars, but others, like his own, had been put to other purposes. Several had been abandoned and were waiting for a strong wind to blow them down. As they passed the slumping shell of one of these, Simon glanced up the lane and froze.

Caesar was nosing around the double doors of his garage. It was no longer the frisky pup Abbey had petted in the park, but the fearsome creature he'd seen from the study window. As though catching wind of his fear, the dog suddenly stopped what it was doing and turned to face them. It fixed them with a glare, and the hackles bristled on the back of its neck. Though it was halfway down the lane, Simon heard the menacing growl that started up in its throat as clearly as he had when it sounded from the bushes that day in the Hawkins yard.

"Don't run," said Abbey. "Back away—slowly."

They began to back up on trembling legs, their feet slipping on the gravelly ground. The dog let out two sharp barks and sank into a crouch. Simon scanned the yards to either side, searching for an escape.

But then, as if in response to some inaudible command, the dog suddenly sat down on its haunches in front of the garage doors and was utterly still. Only its great eyes moved, fixed on their every step as they backed slowly away.

There was a muffled sound of breaking glass that seemed to come from inside the garage. They watched in amazement as a large, dark splotch began to seep out from under the garage doors and creep slowly along the ground till it reached the spot where the dog sat.

Immediately it stood up. With one last look their way, it turned and started off in the opposite direction down the lane. The black shape slid along in front of it, stretching out like pulled toffee into a lean, distended head and two spindly arms and legs—a shadow with a human shape, gliding before the dog as it bounded down the lane, crossed the road, and loped up the walk to the Loudon house.

They stood watching until it was out of sight. Then, with a quick goodbye, Abbey took off along the lane, while Simon hurried toward the back gate of the house.

He slipped into the yard and opened the garage door. It was darker than night inside. As he groped around for the light switch in the dark he felt the telling crunch of shattered glass underfoot. He pictured a scene of devastation around him—things pulled down from their perches, boxes torn open and overturned, the floor strewn with scattered books and papers.

He was far too tired to face it now. He locked the garage behind him and let himself into the house by the back door. Dragging himself up the stairs to his room, he dropped into bed. In moments, he was asleep.

34

Most mornings, they met in the park and walked together to school. No matter how grim he felt, it was better than staying home, staring uneasily across the street as they waited for Cameron's call. At lunch, they huddled together at a corner table in the cafeteria, talking in hushed tones.

With the weather growing cooler, Alice Loudon had abandoned the porch. The car had disappeared from the drive, the dog from the yard. Simon had seen no sign of James Loudon for weeks. The house sat dark and still. Were it not for the steady trickle of students to the door, he would have sworn it was empty.

One Saturday, late in September, Mom was called in to sub for a sick cashier, and Simon was left to babysit Babs. After her afternoon nap, he zipped her into her fall jacket and took her out to the backyard to play while he cut the grass.

His gaze wandered repeatedly to the door of the garage as he worked. He remembered the scene that had met him inside, the day after the trip to the museum. He had expected to encounter devastation, but aside from the wind chime having been knocked down from its nail, shattering several of its chimes on the hard dirt floor, everything was as it had been.

Yet there was an unsettling sense of intrusion to the place, the eerie feeling that something had passed secretly over things, slipped silently down through the gaps between boxes, and slid inside each one.

Babs had brought two of her dolls out with her. She walked them up and down the yard in their toy stroller while he raked and bagged the grass clippings. As the sun sank lower in the sky their shadows stretched long and lean across the lawn. And he thought of other shadows—the one that had seeped out from under the garage door, the one that eased slowly across the museum floor. Suddenly, every shadow took on human shape.

"Let's go in, Babs," he said. "Mama will be home soon."

It had grown chillier since the shadows claimed the yard, and Babs put up little fuss over going in. She scooped up her dolls, and they headed back inside the house.

Omens of autumn were in the air. The dark came down earlier now. The nights were cool, and some of the trees had begun to turn. With the chill came the old ache of illness, the bitter taste on the tongue, the fog in the brain—like a memory stored in the bones. His sleep was shallow, his dreams vivid and strange. He said nothing to anyone, but Abbey knew it was back.

One night the following week, he was up in his room when the doorbell rang. A few minutes later, Mom came to the foot of the stairs and called him down. He heard the piano being played in the background. His breath came short and his heart began to pound. Mom had to call up a second time before he worked up the courage to go down.

"Ah, there you are, Simon," she said as he slunk into the living room. Dad's cigarette was still smoldering in the ashtray. The door to the kitchen was closed. Alice Loudon was seated at the piano, playing.

"Mrs. Loudon has just dropped by to show us the poster she printed up for the fall recital."

Fall recital? It was the first he'd heard of it. Alarm bells began to sound inside him. Alice Loudon glanced up from the piano and gave him a smile.

"Hello, Simon," she said, without a hint in her voice of what lurked just below the surface between them.

She rose to greet him, offering him her gloved hand. As he took it in his he felt bone and sinew strung beneath the cloth—with shocking voids between, where his fingers closed on nothingness. Instinctively, he drew back his hand.

They stood face to face. She wore a jacket with the collar turned up, a silk scarf tied loosely about her neck, a long skirt, high boots. He felt it was no accident that there was not a trace of exposed skin save for her face, which was powdered an ashen white. Her sunglasses perched unsteadily on the bridge of her nose. Her mouth was pulled thin and taut. The flush of her over-painted lips was frightening.

When he plumbed the dark glasses for her eyes, all he saw were still, dark pools.

She reached down and took a handful of posters from a small pile sitting on the coffee table and handed them to him. They were printed in bright fall colors. The old piano that appeared on her business card was scattered now with leaves of brilliant red and burnished gold. FALL RECITAL, it read across the top of the poster. The location and time were printed below.

"Perhaps you could pass some of these around to your friends," she said. "That nice girl I've seen you with. Oh, what's her name?"

"Abbey," offered Mom, when he failed to provide the name.

"Yes, of course—*Abbey*. Perhaps you and Abbey could post a few at school. Everyone is welcome."

"I'm just a bundle of nerves," said Mom. "I've never played in public before. Not like Simon. He's an old pro. Aren't you, dear?"

"No, not really," he said.

"Nonsense. You're just being modest. He won that cup there on the mantel."

"*Mom*," he said.

"There are still a couple of openings for our little recital," said Alice Loudon. "Perhaps we could entice you to come out of retirement."

"I don't think so," he said.

"He's *very* good," said Mom. "A natural—like my dad. He puts me to shame."

"Mustn't hide your light beneath a bushel, Simon,"

said Mrs. Loudon. "I'd love to hear you. Perhaps you could play a little something for me now."

"I haven't played in ages," he said as Alice Loudon steered him toward the piano with the light pressure of her hand. "I don't have any music."

"Why don't you play that little Bach piece Granddad used to play," said Mom, who knew he had the piece by heart. "I'll just be in the kitchen." And off she went.

He sat down reluctantly at the keyboard. It had been more than two years, and he was sure he'd forgotten everything. But with the gentle pressure of Alice Loudon's gloved hand on his shoulder, it was as if a sluice opened inside him. The music flowed freely through him. He had never played so well. He found himself in a place beyond all thought, beyond all doubt and hesitation. His fingers found the keys by themselves.

He felt her hand tighten on his shoulder, felt the power flow from her to him, from him to her, in a steady stream until, by the time the last note sounded, he had lost all sense of self.

"That was splendid," said Mrs. Loudon. "Absolutely splendid." There was a flush of color in her pallid cheeks, a flare of fire in the dark of her eyes. "I do hope you'll play for me again."

Mom reappeared from the kitchen. He was so drained it was all he could do to say his goodbyes and stumble up the stairs to his room.

His sleep that night was full of strange dreams. He saw a masked figure whirling beneath the moon in the Loudons' yard. Come morning, he could still feel Alice Loudon's grip on his shoulder. When he looked in the mirror, the bruised skin bore the imprint of her hand.

He found himself seated at the piano. He had no idea how he got there or how long he'd been playing. Off in the distance a doorbell was ringing. He had a vague feeling it had been ringing for some time. He went to answer it, thinking it might be her. But it was only Abbey.

Abbey took one look at him and knew something was wrong. Hustling him into the kitchen, she splashed cold water on his face. There was still some coffee in the pot Mom had made that morning. Abbey poured him a cup. It was bitter and strong but he bolted it down and it brought him around.

"What's going on, Simon?" she said. "What's happened to you?"

He told her about Alice Loudon's visit, how wonderful it had been playing for her, how incredibly at one with her he'd felt while he played. He told her about the dream of the masked figure dancing beneath the moon.

"Listen to me, Simon," she said, giving him a shake. "You can't let her in here when you're alone. Do you understand?"

He nodded mechanically, but he couldn't see what she was so excited about. His thoughts were all foggy. The only time he felt at all clear was when he was playing. And then it wasn't the music he heard. It was her voice in his head.

It was all he could do to keep his eyes open now. As soon as she left he lay down on the couch and went to sleep.

The next morning, Abbey skipped school. She was on his doorstep at nine sharp and stayed with him the whole day. She forced him to eat something, and kept him away from the piano. The phone rang repeatedly. They let it go to the answering machine, but no message was ever left. The doorbell chimed more than a dozen times. She refused to let him answer it. They peeked through a crack in the drawn curtains as Alice Loudon made her way slowly down the walk and across the street to the old house.

Abbey came back the next day, and the next as well. By then, Simon had begun to feel more like himself. He could still feel the piano calling him, but nowhere near as powerfully as before. He looked in the bathroom mirror and saw himself for the first time in days.

Abbey noticed the difference right away. "Welcome back, Simon," she said. "I called Cameron last night and told her what was going on. She wants us to meet her at a diner down near the museum tomorrow afternoon."

"Remember," she said as she was leaving. "Don't answer the phone. And *don't* let her in."

She hadn't been gone more than five minutes when the phone began to ring. It took every ounce of strength he had in him not to pick it up.

35

The rush hour traffic was hopelessly snarled. Horns blared and brakes squealed. The rain beat against the windows of the bus and drummed on the roof as it crept along. Already running late, Abbey and Simon got off and walked the last few blocks in the rain, sharing Abbey's broken umbrella.

The busy downtown street was a wind tunnel of office towers. People hurried by, battling their umbrellas, clutching their hats. Shop windows snatched their reflections as they passed.

As they approached the diner they saw Cameron's bike chained to a lamppost out front. She was huddled in a back booth, a cup of coffee cradled in her hands. She looked up and waved through the steamy window.

Several people who would normally have been out panhandling on the busy corners had sought refuge in the diner during the downpour. They sat nursing cups of coffee, their belongings bundled beside them. They glanced up with guarded eyes as Simon and Abbey blew in with a rush of wind out of the rain.

Cameron stood to greet them as they came dripping down the aisle. Her clothes had a slept-in look about them. Slack tendrils of hair hung from her bun. She tucked them briskly behind her ear as she sat back down. Her backpack and bicycle helmet lay on the bench beside her.

Simon and Abbey sat down in the booth, facing her. The waitress tore herself away from the TV and ambled over to take their order. Cameron ordered the all-day breakfast; Simon and Abbey ordered colas and a plate of fries. While they waited, Cameron asked Simon to tell her about Alice Loudon's visit to the house.

He struggled to find words for the feeling he'd had of power flowing between them as she laid her hand on his shoulder while he played for her. Just talking about it woke the longing again. He told her about the fatigue that had followed, the strange dreams, the deep fog that had settled over him.

"You should have seen the shape I found him in the day after her visit," said Abbey. "He's better now, but she keeps phoning, and knocking on the door. It's only a matter of time before she worms her way in. And it's not just him she's affected."

Simon told Cameron about the changes he'd seen in his mom and the other adults and kids in the neighborhood since they started taking lessons with Alice Loudon.

The waitress reappeared with their food. Cameron tucked into hers right away, eating ravenously. She looked up and saw their stares.

"Forgive me," she said. "I've been sleeping in my office since you brought me the mirror, catching meals when I can. I didn't think it wise to leave it alone." She spoke of hearing strange noises in the hall at night, the furtive rattling of the door handle at all hours.

"Perhaps it's just my imagination—but I've taken protective measures all the same." Reaching under the neck of her sweater she pulled out a band of cloth covered in hieroglyphic symbols that she was wearing round her neck.

"It's an ancient spell," she explained. "Egyptian magicians often wrote spells on strips of cloth to be worn by those in need of protection."

She took two short strips of linen covered in hieroglyphics from her pocket. "I've prepared these for you," she said. "They're to be worn around your wrist and left there till they fall away. After what you've told me, I think you may need them."

Folding the strips lengthwise, she tied several elaborate knots in each. "The knots form a barrier the evil forces are unable to pass," she said.

Leaning across the table, she tied the cloth securely around their wrists, chanting the words of the spell as she did. Several people swung their heads around to see what on earth was going on in the back booth as Abbey and Simon tucked the bracelets out of sight under their sleeves.

Cameron reached into her backpack and brought out a strange-looking object. It was about two feet long, flat, and curved like a boomerang, decorated on both sides with crudely drawn human and animal figures. One end had been honed into a point, blunted with wear. It was clearly an ancient thing.

As she handed it to Simon he felt it thrum with pent-up power. He set it down quickly on the table. It lay among the cups and plates and cutlery like something from another world. Abbey reached out and ran her fingers over the scratched-in figures of snakes and jackals and animal-headed humans.

"It's called an apotropaic wand," said Cameron. "It's made from hippopotamus tusk, and shaped like the throw sticks ancient Egyptians used for hunting birds. Magicians used it to draw magic circles around those they wished to keep safe from the evil forces that flocked like birds about them. I've written down a spell to accompany it." And she handed him a piece of folded paper.

"Now this is what I want you to do later tonight, Simon," she said. As she leaned across the table and whispered her instructions to him, he felt as if they'd left the world of office towers and traffic jams far behind and entered into an ancient realm, where the forces of good and evil were locked in endless battle.

He remembered the poster he'd brought with him. "I wanted to show you this," he said, taking it from his pocket and handing it to her. "It's for a fall concert Alice Loudon is planning."

Cameron examined it closely. "Does this look familiar

to you?" she said, pointing to the undulating line that framed the poster.

"That's the pattern that runs around the rim of the mirror," said Abbey, and Simon suddenly realized it was.

"Music played a vital role in ancient magic," said Cameron. "It was believed that music drove off evil powers. So spells were often sung or chanted to the accompaniment of rattles or clappers or rhythmic stamping. If an ancient Egyptian magician were somehow translated to the modern world, it would make perfect sense that she would appear as a musician.

"After what you've told me about your recent encounter with Alice Loudon, and the changes you've noticed in her pupils, I wonder if she might somehow be sustaining her own life by feeding on the lives of others through music. She may see this recital as a means of restoring her failing powers by drawing on the lives of all those gathered there. Who knows where that may lead?"

"But how can we stop her?" said Abbey. "Even in the state she's in now, we're no match for her. Look what she did to Simon."

"We have to find a way to exploit her limitations," said Cameron. "In the end, she's a reflection, a shadow, a two-dimensional being in a three-dimensional world. She's a creature of surfaces. She lacks depth, imagination. She's unable to read another's thoughts, to imagine hidden motives. Those who possess these qualities are able to deceive her—as you were able to hide your knowledge of the whereabouts of the mirror from her when she asked you about it, Simon. In addition, she's desperate, and because of that may become reckless and leave herself vulnerable."

The waitress came with more coffee. She filled Cameron's cup and cleared away the empty plates. When she'd left, Cameron leaned forward, resting her arms on the table.

"I have a plan," she said. "A plan to call her back into the mirror, where she can do no further harm. We will lay a trap for her and lure her in. It will take all three of us to carry it off, but we must be patient and wait for just the right time. The eye engraved on the mirror is the eye of Horus, the falcon-headed god. It's a potent protective symbol, identified with the moon. At its full, the moon is a powerful force for magic. We had a new moon last night. Two Fridays from now it will be full again. That's when we'll act."

They sat huddled together over the table as Cameron unpacked her plan. By the time they were done, the rain had stopped and dusk had fallen. Most of the other customers in the diner had drifted off, and the waitress was looking up at the clock. They paid the bill and left.

"Be careful. And remember—not a word of our plan to anyone," said Cameron as she unlocked her bike and strapped on her helmet. "And don't forget what you're to do tonight, Simon."

The wheels hissed like snakes against the wet road, and the bike light flashed like a beacon as she drove off into the dark.

The downtown windows blared with light. Reflections lurked everywhere. Even the roads were riddled with mirrors after the rain. Abbey and Simon veered off the main drag to the refuge of quieter streets. Each lost in their own thoughts, they threaded their way silently home.

Late that night, Simon slipped out of his bedroom window and stole across the porch roof. He scrambled down the shaky trellis. Across the road the Loudon house was dark. The street was still. A sliver of moon hung in the sky.

Starting at the base of the trellis, he worked his way down the alley, through the gap in the fence into his yard and then across it, scratching a line on the ground behind him with the point of the ivory wand and reciting the words of the spell Cameron had given him:

> *The eye of Horus lights the way,*
> *Through dark of night it shines like day.*
> *Begone, you spirits. With this wand*
> *I set a bound upon your harm.*
> *These words of Magic from my mouth—*
> *By East, by West, by North, by South—*
> *Arouse the gods carved on this knife,*
> *And each one leaps out into life,*
> *And armed about this circle goes,*
> *To drive away all deadly foes.*

He stole silently up the walk on the other side of the house and across the front lawn, drawing the wand along the ground behind him. It made a whispery, rustling sound, as if the creatures inscribed upon it had leapt free and walked in his footsteps.

Begone, you spirits who do ill,
I seal this circle with a spell.
You shall not harm those in this house—
By East, by West, by North, by South.

At the foot of the trellis he touched the end of the magic circle to the beginning and closed it. It crackled and flared for an instant like a downed wire, and then went dark. He scurried back up the trellis and slipped inside through the open window.

Sleep came swiftly—deep and dreamless.

36

"**P**hone for you, Simon," Mom called up the stairs.

He plopped down on the edge of the bed and picked up the receiver.

"Hello."

"Hello, Simon. It's Cameron. Can you talk?"

"Yes," he said. "This is a good time."

"The mirror doesn't feel safe in my office anymore. I think I've found the perfect solution for what to do with it. I'm going to hide it right here in the museum—in plain sight. No one will ever suspect it's there. I'm planning to do it this Friday, after closing."

"Is there anything I can do?"

"No. Just sit tight. I'll call you when it's done."

There was a click on the line as she hung up. A moment later there was another, lighter click on the downstairs line.

After dinner that night, Mom left Dad and him to do the dishes. Tucking her sheet music under her arm, she headed across the street to Alice Loudon's house for one of the special lessons she'd been taking in preparation for the concert. Simon watched through the front window as she disappeared through the door. Later that night, he called Cameron and Abbey.

It was late Friday night. The full moon hung high in a cloudless sky. It peeped through the tall lancet windows of the museum as Cameron passed though the silent gallery, the beam of her flashlight panning over the dark display cases.

A scattering of security lights picked out a scene or two. One shone down on the mummy case, another on the diorama of the Egyptian woman doing her makeup. She was applying a dark line of kohl to her eyelids with a pointed ivory stick as she gazed in the mirror in her hand.

The mirror was much like the one Cameron carried with her. As she approached the case, she switched off the flashlight and set it down on the floor. Taking a small key from her pocket, she slid it into the lock on the side of the case. There was a faint *click* as the catch was released, and the front panel swung open.

With the wall of glass gone, everything changed. The impenetrable barrier between past and present, imagined and real, was suddenly removed. The relationship between herself and this achingly lifelike figure from antiquity was instantly altered. No longer was it the living on one side, the lifeless on the other; the two had magically merged. As she looked at her, Cameron imagined Alice Loudon as she might have looked back then.

As she reached into the case to exchange the mirror in the mannequin's hand for that in hers, she heard the whisper of claws against the wooden floor. Glancing over her shoulder, she saw a large black jackal-like dog slide from the shadows on the far side of the room, fixing her with its baleful eyes.

There was a faint rustle from the shadows behind it. And slowly, as though spun from shadow itself, a second figure emerged. It was Alice Loudon.

"So we meet at last," she said.

Cameron looked her full in the face without flinching. She felt she knew this woman. She had prepared for this moment, and now the creature of her imaginings stood before her in the flesh.

It was a figure from another time and place. She wore a linen sheath, belted at the waist. Her hair and makeup were in the Egyptian style. About her neck hung the missing necklace, fashioned from beads of gold and colored glass, with amulets of polished stone strung between. In her hand she held the missing snake wand—a bronze cobra with bared fangs.

For a moment, she seemed to falter under Cameron's steady gaze. But then she fastened on the mirror, and desire flared in her dead eyes.

"Give me my mirror," she said.

"I think not," said Cameron. Straightening to her full height, she stepped back and faced her adversary full on.

"You are a fool, and you will suffer for your insolence," said Alice Loudon. "Before we are finished here, you will beg me to take it from you." And she threw down the wand.

It resounded like thunder as it struck the floor, and was instantly transformed. Its rigidity dissolved into undulating waves, and it slithered swiftly across the shadowed room toward Cameron. Suddenly, it reared up. Its tongue flicked and its hood flared as it swayed hypnotically from side to side, preparing to strike.

Cameron stood her ground. Holding the mirror before her in her outstretched hands, she chanted the words of an ancient spell. Mesmerized by its reflection, the creature reared back and struck hard against the surface of the mirror with a sound like the clash of swords, and fell lifeless to the floor. Cameron kicked it with the toe of her shoe, and it clattered up against the display case, again a harmless wand.

"Ah, a formidable opponent," said Alice Loudon. "How refreshing. And she even speaks the old tongue, however strangely.

"Very well. You've had your fun. Now be a good woman and give me the mirror, or I promise you your fun will come to a sudden end." She let her hand fall to her side, where the dog stood motionless as a statue. Now its eyes flared, and the hackles bristled on the back of its neck. "Don't be a fool," she said. "Of what possible use could the old thing be to you? If it's mirrors you want, I have a house full of them—some of them quite valuable, I believe. Just give me this one." And she took a measured step toward her. "It does belong to me, you know."

"Yes, I know it does, Mrs. Loudon. Or should I call you Mereret?"

A shudder ran through Alice Loudon, like a flame struck by a sudden gust of wind.

"It was millennia ago I last heard that name," she said. "Even in my lifetime it was closely guarded lest it fall into evil hands and put me in their power. But you know that, don't you? What else, I wonder, do you know?"

She took another step and came within the glow of one of the security lights.

"What *can* you know, shut in this little sliver of light you call life? You are like a cat following a stray beam of sunlight about the house to lie down in and doze awhile. What can you possibly know of the lust for life, the thrill of breath in the lungs, the dance of blood in the veins, you who tend dead things?

"But come, come, let us not quarrel. Just give me my mirror. What will you do with it? Measure it? Label it? Set it in some dismal case among all these other dusty, drained things? It's *nothing* to you. To me, it's—"

"Life itself," said Cameron.

Alice Loudon looked at her steadily and long.

"Yes," she said at last, "life itself." The admission cost her dearly. Some vital force in her briefly lost its hold, and for a moment, she seemed a sad, broken thing. But she rallied and went on:

"I never dreamt it would be so when fate first freed me from the mirror, and I leapt into life. Not the bounded world of that bronze prison, the flat world of reflection. But *Life*—in three glorious dimensions. Unbounded being. The freedom, the fullness, the bliss of it. The before, behind, above, below of it. The thrill of touch, of solidity, of depth. All of it spread out like untold riches around me.

"I had known magic, felt its awesome power, commanded

it when I could, to heal the sick, to shatter the forces of evil and trample them underfoot. But never had I known magic such as this. I thought it would be mine forever.

"I left the mirror far behind me, like a prisoner leaves the cell she has fled. I merged seamlessly with the world. I possessed every key, opened every door. Wealth and power were at my command. Others aged about me; the strong grew frail, the high were brought low. The living passed before me like shadows on a wall. But I remained—untouched by time, unchanged, unchangeable.

"And when suspicion cast its eye upon me, I took flight, and built my nest in a new place. The world in all its splendor was mine. I spread my arms wide and took it in my embrace. Music was my love, then as now. I mastered the piano with ease. My skill opened doors. I played to packed halls, had audiences with royalty. I took no thought of the mirror—where it might have gone, whose hands it may have fallen into. It was of no more use to me than the cast-off slough to the snake that has burst its bonds.

"But then—slowly at first, so slowly as to be almost imperceptible—mortality found me out, like a hunter its prey. A weariness came upon me where there had been none before. Pain set its hooks in me: an ache that would not pass, a wound that would not heal, a scar that left its lingering stamp.

"My grip on this world grew weaker day by day. I would fall without warning into the realm of shadows, the flat-land of reflection, the land of living death. Suddenly darkness brought terrors. Abysses yawned beneath me.

"I began to dream. I dreamt ceaselessly of the mirror.

Soon I could think of little else. It seemed to me my salvation. If only I found it again, I told myself, all would be well. I would plunge into its pure, bright pool and be made new.

"I searched far and wide for it, but it eluded me always. And then, some years back, it turned up unexpectedly at auction. I stood so close to it I could stroke it with my hand, lean down and look into its magical depths. But it slipped through my fingers—and was gone."

She stopped abruptly, blinked and looked about, suddenly aware of having betrayed more of herself than she meant.

"But enough of this prattle," she boomed. "I have found it again. And this time I will have it." She stamped upon the ground and took another step toward Cameron.

Again the words that came from Cameron's mouth were in the ancient tongue as she stooped and described a circle around the place where she stood with the mirror's edge.

"Match magic with me, would you?" said Alice Loudon scornfully. "I have filled my belly with magic. Spells spring from my mouth."

She reached down and with a touch of her hand released the dog from where it stood spellbound by her side. It let out a horrific growl and lunged with lightning speed across the room. As it neared the spot where Cameron stood, it sprang into the air.

Cameron held the mirror out before her at arm's length, bracing it with both hands. Light streamed from it like a second sun. The edge of it caught the beast flush on the throat in mid-flight. For a long moment, it hung suspended in the air, and then it dropped like a stone to the floor.

It lay there motionless as darkness pooled around it like a shadow. As the life ebbed from it, the shape shifted. Now it was no longer the dog that lay there, but James Loudon, curled on his side as if asleep. Then that shape shifted also, and in its place a small clay figure in the form of a black jackal; a magical protector animated by means of a spell. She brought her foot down on it and crushed it to pieces, destroying its power.

Alice Loudon looked down at the shattered thing without a trace of emotion. "I have had that a good many years," she said. "It will cost me pains to replace it. You will pay for this."

And she took another step toward her.

37

Meanwhile, tucked out of sight behind the mummy case on the far side of the room, two figures had silently observed all. Abbey gazed awestruck as the pool of shadow spread around the fallen dog and the figure of James Loudon appeared in its place. And Simon saw something in Alice Loudon's face he'd never seen before—a faint flicker of doubt, as if something she had not imagined possible had occurred. In a moment, it was gone.

As she advanced ever closer toward Cameron, she seemed to swell in size and power. Her eyes were dark pools. Everything that came within their compass was caught as though in the grip of a deadly whirlpool.

Simon drew his eyes away and peered through the glass of the case at the mummy, sunk in its profound sleep. Once he had found it terrifying, but now her quiet slumber helped calm him. As he crouched behind the case, awaiting their cue, he felt the precious paper in his hand, and the oft-rehearsed words began to sound in his head like the steady beating of a drum.

Cameron stood her ground by the open case with the mirror in her hand. It shone with a steady inward light that bathed the room in its glow.

"Give me my mirror," Alice Loudon demanded again.

"You will have to take it."

"I will drain your life and leave you a shadow."

"As you are a shadow," Cameron replied.

Alice Loudon's eyes flashed fire. She took another step, and her toe touched the edge of the magic circle. There was an ominous crackling as it sparked with bridled power.

"Quite close enough, I think," said Cameron.

Holding the mirror before her she began to chant the words of the spell she had crafted from the ancient texts. The air thrummed, and the lights flickered.

> *Mereret, I know your name.*
> *I bind your powers in Magic's chains.*
> *Your feet I root into the earth.*
> *Your limbs grow slack as babes' at birth.*
> *Your words I shackle in your mouth,*
> *By East, by West, by North, by South...*

As the words rained down on her like blows, Alice Loudon recoiled.

Cameron had hoped the spell would so take her by surprise that the full incantation would go uncontested. She had enlisted Simon and Abbey's aid, teaching them the words of power, to prepare for what might happen if it did not.

"My magic is a mighty..."

As she attempted to continue the incantation, her eyes locked with Alice Loudon's. She felt her adversary's power surge through her, weakening her resolve and leaving her limp. Suddenly, the weight of the mirror was unbearable. It was all she could do to hold it out before her. As her strength failed, the words of the spell deserted her.

Alice Loudon watched the panic creep into her eyes.

"A valiant effort," she said. "But you will learn to your sorrow that magic is more than words pillaged from the pages of old books. It is life—and power."

She boldly breached the magic circle as if it were no more than a chalk figure some child had scrawled on the ground. But as she reached to take the mirror, Cameron stepped back and turned toward the mummy case.

This was their cue. Simon and Abbey stepped from behind the shelter of the case and showed themselves.

"You!" said Alice Loudon.

Simon raised the trembling paper in his hands. Together he and Abbey took up the words of the spell. Cameron drew renewed strength from them and joined in:

> My Magic is a mighty storm
> That blows you back where you belong.
> Behold the portal, open wide.
> Your home lies on the farther side.
> The eye of Horus shows the way
> From darkness into realms of day.

The circle flared, and Alice Loudon shrank back outside its bounds. Her gaze flitted back and forth between them, and her hands flew to her ears, attempting to block out the words of the spell. But the very walls seemed to sound with them now.

The mirror blazed like the desert sun, and a tremor ran through the room, rattling the artifacts in their cases like dishes on a tray.

She stood rooted to the spot, her slack form swaying to and fro like a tree in a storm.

> *By Hekah, Horus, Thoth and Bes,*
> *By North, by South, by East, by West,*
> *By all who breathe this mortal breath,*
> *Begone back to the land of death.*

As the final words were uttered, a strange expression stole over Alice Loudon's face—part terror and part rapture. And she was lifted up like a thing spun from smoke and shadow, and sucked with a long, keening cry into the mirror.

It flared briefly and then went dark as a dull green cast flowed over its surface, quenching its light. Cameron dropped it with a clang to the floor and stood rubbing her hands together and blowing into them. Silence settled over the room, a silence so deep they could hear the beating of their hearts.

Simon and Abbey drifted over to Cameron's side. The three stood looking mutely down at the mirror. No more was it the object of gleaming bronze that had drawn Simon down into its magical depths, but an ancient artifact like those ranged about it, its face shrouded with corrosion like a pond sheathed in ice.

All that remained of Alice Loudon was a bronze wand, capped with a cobra's head, and an ancient necklace that had snapped as it fell and scattered its amulets and beads like seeds across the shadowed floor.

38

He was taking dinner to Mr. Hawkins. It was a gorgeous summer day. The smell of lemon pudding cake wafted up from the tray as he crossed the street and started up the Hawkins walk. The garden was vibrant with color, and the wisteria was in bloom. The wind chime tinkled a tune in greeting as he came up the stairs. He gave the bell a twist and heard it trill brightly in the hallway beyond the door.

"Come in, Simon," called a faint voice.

He gave the door a nudge and went in. A vase of fresh roses stood on the table at the foot of the stairs, filling the hall with their scent. The mirrors cradled his reflection as he went by.

Turning into the front room, he saw the TV table drawn up before the old man's empty chair. As he set the tray down he noticed differences everywhere. The clutter that had covered the dining room table had disappeared, and the camp cot stood with folded wings in the corner. Where the Egyptian mirror had hung, there was now a print of a ship at sea. The TV had been wheeled forward and turned on, but the blizzard in which the broadcaster always delivered his news had passed, and the picture was clear.

A sudden thud overhead set the ceiling fixture trembling. He heard the sound of something heavy being hauled along the upstairs hall.

"Give me a hand with this, will you, Simon? It weighs a ton."

Hurrying to the foot of the stairs, he saw Mr. Hawkins standing at the top with the large old suitcase that had stood at the foot of the bed. It bulged like a ripe seedpod with whatever had been crammed inside. Together, they bumped it down the stairs into the hall.

Mr. Hawkins straightened and ran a hankie over his forehead. "I've no idea what Eleanor's got in there. She packs like she's never coming back. Perhaps she knows something I don't," he said with a laugh.

Simon got a good look at him now for the first time. He was awestruck. All traces of the old man he knew had vanished, and in their place stood the young man in the photos on the wall, his muscles lean and firm, his face trim and tanned.

He smiled down at Simon. "I won't be needing you to bring me dinner anymore," he said. "I'm off on a new dig. Very exciting. It promises to be a fabulously rich find. Eleanor's gone on ahead, and I'm to meet her there. No telling when we'll be back. I trust you'll look after things here for me while we're gone."

He extended a strong calloused hand to Simon. "Thank you for everything," he said. "I could never have managed without you." Hefting the heavy suitcase, he swayed beneath its weight as he walked down the hall.

He opened the front door, and the hall was flooded with brilliant light.

"Cab's waiting," he said. " I must be going."

He turned to leave, then suddenly turned back. "By the way," he said, and the light seemed to stream from his silhouetted form as he stood in the doorway. "Be sure to take good care of that book I gave you. It may be worth something someday." And he drew the door closed behind him, and was gone.

Simon woke with a start in the sunlit room and glanced at the clock. He'd dozed off for a few minutes at most, though the dream had gone on and on. It was with him still—so achingly real he could have reached out and touched it. His heart raced with the strangeness of it, and he was filled with such a sense of peace that he was afraid to stir, lest it fade.

He lay unmoving on the bed, and his eyes roamed the room. Precarious piles crowned every piece of furniture—the lingering landscape of illness. He was looking for one thing in particular. Something he'd forgotten in the mad whirl of events that followed Mr. Hawkins' death: the book of prints the old man had sent him as a get-well gift the week before he died. His eye fell on the spine of it now, peeking out from under the pile of old archaeological journals.

Crossing the room, he eased it carefully out and carried it to his bed. He'd no sooner started to fan through it than it fell open at the print he'd seen hanging on the wall in the dream. Two sheets of folded paper had been tucked in the book at that spot. The moment he opened them, he recognized the old man's writing.

It was the missing will.

Max and Babs were buzzing around the dessert table like bees at a picnic. Decked out in their Sunday best, they looked like a pair of angels—but they had mischief on their minds. At the moment, they were off in the corner conspiring, pointing toward the table as they planned their next assault. They'd skipped straight from toddlerhood to juvenile delinquency.

"Aren't they just darling?" said a woman in pink with pearl earrings who had clearly never chased children around a dessert table at a social gathering.

Simon sidled over to Babs. Dipping one corner of his napkin in his tea, he dropped to his haunches and made a quick stab at her chocolatey face before she could dart away. The instant she squirmed free, she made a beeline for the dessert table with her partner in crime.

He plopped down in one of the rows of folding chairs that had been set up at one end of the small room. It was a Sunday afternoon in May at the museum, and he was on Babs patrol. Six months had passed since the fateful night he'd last set foot in the museum. The circumstances were much different now than then.

It was the official opening of the Hawkins Collection of Early Mirrors. As he glanced around he saw the many mirrors he'd come to know in the months he carried dinner to Mr. Hawkins, plucked from their accustomed places and set side by side in tall glass cases lining the walls of the room. Each woke a memory, opened a door onto a past still present. He felt that if he were to stand and stare through the glass at any one of them now, he would meet the reflection he'd cast back then, and be transported there again.

Mom and Dad were on the far side of the room, talking to Cameron. Babs had brought them plunder from the dessert table. According to the provisions of the Hawkins' will, the mirror collection had been bequeathed to the museum under the care of Dr. Cameron. The old house itself, much to their amazement, had been left to Simon's family.

In a note appended to the will, Mr. Hawkins had written:

I have lived in this house since I was a child. It was passed on to me when my parents died, and it was here Eleanor and I lived throughout our married life. It is a place so steeped in memory that it is almost a living thing. The ghosts of days long gone throng about me. With no children or family to pass it on to, it has troubled me more than I can say to think of it all coming to an end.

All that changed the day I fell from the ladder and you, dear Jenny, came to my rescue and took me into your care. I am more grateful than I can say for the kindness you and your family have shown me. I am especially grateful to you, Simon, who have made me see how much I have missed, and have helped amend that loss. It is a great joy to be able to share the passion for the things one loves— and to find one so eager to learn is greater still.

And so I leave this house to you, in memory of those days, so long ago, when two boys sat side by side on the porch steps and dreamt of all the world might hold. It held all of that—and so much more.

A hush fell over the room as Cameron rose to speak. Babs crawled up on the empty seat next to Mom and nestled up against her. Mom was back to her old self again. Her time with Alice Loudon had taken, on for her, the quality of a dream.

Slowly, in the weeks and months that had intervened since then, the neighborhood had also revived. The Loudons themselves—from their auspicious arrival on the street to their sudden mysterious disappearance—had already begun to pass into neighborhood lore.

"Kind friends and colleagues," said Cameron, "it is with great pleasure that I welcome you today to the official unveiling of the Hawkins Collection of Early Mirrors, a remarkable bequest to the museum by the noted archaeologist Randall Hawkins. Over the years, he and his wife Eleanor patiently assembled the splendid collection you see around you here, a collection that encapsulates the history and development of the mirror down the centuries.

"I once asked Professor Hawkins what it was about mirrors that drew him so powerfully to them. He told me that it was not simply the mirrors themselves, beautiful though they were, but the mystery they held in their depths, a mystery that moved ancient people to awe and wonder..."

Despite his best intentions, Simon found it all too much. His health was slowly improving, but his emotions were still skewed, and the least thing could set him off. He wandered off now before tears flowed and he made a fool of himself.

Recently, he'd been back to see Dad's mountain-climbing doctor, who'd been able to shed new light on his illness. Since Simon had been to see him, he'd had another case of the same mysterious ailment come through his door—a young woman in her twenties, a distance runner, suddenly laid low with all the same symptoms. News of the baffling syndrome had begun to surface in the medical literature. A wave of similar cases had been reported recently on the west coast—perfectly well people suddenly afflicted by an elusive ailment that compromised their immune systems, and caused debilitating fatigue and impaired cognitive function.

They called it myalgic encephalomyelitis—ME for short. The doctor had copied an article with case studies of kids Simon's age who'd fallen victim to it. Their stories were eerily like his. There was speculation in the medical community that the underlying cause was a 'stealth virus' affecting the brain, perhaps triggered by sensitivity to one or more of the many new chemicals introduced into the environment in recent years. There was no known cure but rest and time.

He was not the old Simon—not by a long shot. The slightest stress would plunge him instantly back, the changing of the seasons suddenly waken the sleeping beast again. But, somehow, having a name to put to it, and knowing that others also struggled with the mystery of it, made him feel less alone.

According to Abbey's dad, diseases like ME had been recorded down through history, the earliest dating back to ancient Egypt.

He often wondered what connection there might have been between his illness and events surrounding the Egyptian mirror. Not that the mirror had caused his illness; he'd been unwell before he ever saw it. And when it was at its worst, the mirror was hidden in the frozen ground in Mr. Hawkins' garden.

But perhaps the mystery of the illness had opened him to other mysteries, had made him more receptive to the mirror's magic than he would have been otherwise. Sickness had snatched him from the day-to-day world and dropped him into a night country, where primitive forces were still at play beneath the surface of things.

The opening ceremony had extended long past closing time, and the museum was deserted. He drifted like a ghost through the darkened gallery. He settled in front of a display of metalwork from the late Middle Ages, drawn to a small silver mirror that formed part of a toiletry set for travelers. There were glass mirrors at the time, Mr. Hawkins said in his book, but the quality of the glass was poor and the reflections were flawed. People called them shadowface mirrors, and preferred the metal ones.

He had passed the "Soul Catchers" manuscript on to Cameron, who had recently found a publisher for it. He'd asked if he could have the manuscript back when they were done. It had become part of him.

Abbey came up quietly behind him, her reflection joining his in the glass.

"Are you all right, Simon?"

"Yeah, I'm fine."

"Feel like a walk?"

"Yeah."

As they drifted off through the gallery, their reflections leapt from case to case and Cameron's voice dwindled to a murmur in the distance.

They emerged at last onto the landing. Without either of them saying a word, they started up the stairs. The centuries sloughed away, and they stood again at the top, at the entrance to the Egyptian Gallery. A deep silence had settled over all, as though the very building held its breath.

They passed slowly through the shadowed gallery, quietly reclaiming it from the ghosts that inhabited it now. Spears of sunlight crept silently across the creaky floor. Echoes of the spell they'd spoken that night hung like cobwebs in the high corners of the room, too out of reach for time to sweep away.

Outside the mummy room, they paused and peered down into the case containing the magical objects found hidden under the floor of the dwelling in the pyramid workers' town. Alongside the tattered mask, the ivory clappers, and the small clay figurines, the snake wand lay rigid and still on its velvet bed.

As they entered the mummy room they stared down at the spot where Alice Loudon had last stood. Crossing to the mummy case, they gazed silently through the glass. The mummy slept her long sleep, undisturbed by mortal joys and fears. He saw a peace in her face he had not seen before.

The lid of the coffin hung suspended in the air above her as if by magic. A horizontal band of hieroglyphs ran around all four sides. At the head of the long side, facing him, two eyes were painted on the lid. Standing on tiptoe, he glimpsed the band of hieroglyphs that ran along the top of the lid. It was here, where the name of the deceased was traditionally written, that Cameron had found the magician's name—Mereret. Knowing the name had been crucial to the working of the spell.

They wandered over to the nearby case, where the objects that had been found with the mummy were on display. A shaft of sunlight edged up the side of the case to look in with them. The broken necklace had been restored, and lay in place alongside the collection of amulets that had been found tucked in the mummy's wrappings. But there was a recent addition as well. To make room for it the others had been shifted slightly, so that the dark outlines of their former positions showed like shadows beside them on the sun-bleached velvet.

It was a bronze mirror, about the size of a dinner plate. A green patina of corrosion lay smoothly over its surface, as if it had been dipped in time and transformed. The descriptive card beneath it read simply: *Bronze Mirror, Middle Kingdom, Egypt, c. 1,800 B.C.*

Simon could have filled a book with all it might have said.

Looking down at it now, he remembered his first sight of it hanging on the wall in the front room the day he first brought Mr. Hawkins his dinner. He thought of all that had happened after: the night in the Loudon's yard when Abbey had lifted it free of its shallow grave and held it up gleaming in the moonlight; the vision he'd seen in it of Alice Loudon at the vanity; the final confrontation here, when it had blazed like the sun as Cameron held it before her and the words of the spell resounded through the room. All of it now was part of the mirror's history, part of the mystery sealed beneath its shrouded surface.

For a long while, he thought he knew what had happened that night. Their combined magic had simply proved more powerful than hers. But recently Cameron had wondered aloud if they actually had overcome her. Weak though she was, she said, there had been a force at Alice Loudon's command that surpassed anything they could bring against her. Perhaps it had always been a matter between Alice Loudon and the mirror. And in the end, she had simply allowed herself to be called back home.

"The mirror is an opening in time," said Cameron. "The entrance to a realm we cannot even begin to imagine. Alice Loudon was an immortal being, fallen for a moment into time with all its joy and pain, and then taken back in again."

As he looked down at the eye inscribed on the mirror's face, Simon imagined her standing there now, one eye pressed up against the opening—like the eyes peering out at Cameron through the broken wall. He jerked back.

"What is it?" said Abbey.

"Just a little spooked," he said.

"We should be going," she said. "They'll be wondering where we are."

As they turned and started back his arm brushed the corner of a case, and the frayed bracelet on his wrist snapped and fell with a sigh to the floor. As Abbey stooped to pick it up, he glanced back at the gallery one last time.

MICHAEL BEDARD is a multi-award-winning author of middle-grade and young-adult novels that blend his love of literature with a flair for the ominous. His novels include *A Darker Magic*, *The Green Man*, and *Redwork*, which won the Governor General's Literary Award and the CLA Book of the Year Award for Children. Michael was born and raised in Toronto, where he still lives.

He caught a sudden glint from the case. It was there just a moment, and then it was gone. It was only the sunlight glinting off the glass case, he told himself. But it was all he could do to keep from running back to look down at the mirror again.

"Time to go, Simon," said Abbey.

She took his hand in hers and they turned and walked together out of the gallery. The only sound in the silent room was the whisper of their footsteps on the echoing stairs.